"Live for the moment, Morgen. Hmm?"

His arms sliding seductively round her waist, Conall wished fervently that he could banish every trace of sadness from her beautiful green eyes. He couldn't ever remember feeling that way about any other woman, and he'd dated many.

"So, Miss McKenzie…where do we go from here?"

It was difficult to think straight with the sudden rush of blood to her head. Her expression revealing her anxiety more candidly than she knew, Morgen glanced nervously up at Conall. "Where do you want to go from here?"

He overwhelmed her with another sexy smile, and the strong arms around her waist tightened a little. "Want me to be frank with you?"

Morgen nodded.

"Your bed would be good."

For several years **MAGGIE COX** was a reluctant secretary who dreamed of becoming a published author. She can't remember a time when she didn't have her head in a book or wasn't busy filling exercise books with stories. When she was ten years old her favorite English teacher told her, "If you don't become a writer I'll eat my hat!" But it was only after marrying the love of her life that she finally became convinced she might be able to achieve her dream. Now a self-confessed champion of dreamers everywhere, she urges everyone with a dream to go for it and never give up. Also a busy full-time mom, who tries constantly not to be so busy in what she laughingly calls her spare time, she loves to watch good drama or romantic movies, and eat chocolate!

Maggie Cox

IN HER BOSS'S BED

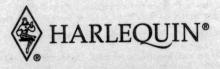

HARLEQUIN®

TORONTO • NEW YORK • LONDON
AMSTERDAM • PARIS • SYDNEY • HAMBURG
STOCKHOLM • ATHENS • TOKYO • MILAN • MADRID
PRAGUE • WARSAW • BUDAPEST • AUCKLAND

To my wonderful brother Billy, loved but not lost.
I will hold you in my heart forever.

ISBN 0-373-18853-6

IN HER BOSS'S BED

First North American Publication 2005.

Copyright © 2004 by Maggie Cox.

This edition published by arrangement with Harlequin Books S.A.

® and TM are trademarks of the publisher. Trademarks indicated with
® are registered in the United States Patent and Trademark Office, the
Canadian Trade Marks Office and in other countries.

www.eHarlequin.com

Printed in U.S.A.

CHAPTER ONE

THE voice in her head seemed to come from far away, and had a sense of urgency about it. Irritated at the interruption to her dream, Morgen mentally willed it away, longing for the dream to come back. But to no avail. It was gone, like leaves scattered by the wind. As the fog in her head began to clear it became painfully apparent that she had pins and needles in her hands—the same hands that her head was resting on, on her desk.

'Oh, my God!'

Lifting her head, she briskly rubbed her palms together, then flexed her fingers, her heart racing slightly as the blood began to circulate again. It started racing even more when she saw the stony-faced expression of the man standing on the other side of the desk, disapproval bracketing a mouth that looked as if it smiled just about as often as Morgen had dinner at the Savoy.

She started to rise to her feet. 'I'm sorry, I—'

'Was wasting the firm's time? By my calculations it's at least another hour until lunch, and I've been told that most of the staff in this office grab a sandwich and eat it at their desk. Obviously you have *other*, less strenuous ideas for using your desk, Miss…?'

Hateful man! For a couple of moments Morgen struggled to get a handle on her anger, not to mention humiliation, but then, taking a deep breath and tucking her hair behind her ear, she straightened her shoulders and rallied. How dared he cast aspersions on her character by insin-

uating that she fell asleep at her desk on a regular basis?
And who, in God's name, was he anyway?

'My falling asleep like that has never happened before,
Mr…?'

'You first.' He ran an impatient hand through hair the
colour of rich dark caramel, and Morgen couldn't help
noticing that he looked in urgent need of both a haircut
and a shave. Besides that, there was an edge about him
that made her stomach knot. This was a man who would
never suffer the indignity of being ignored, she concluded, not in this life. And it wasn't just because of
those jaw-dropping good looks, either.

'McKenzie. Morgen McKenzie.'

'And—apart from being employed by this firm to do
apparently not very much—you work for Derek Holden,
is that right?'

Swallowing with difficulty, Morgen felt the slight burn
of heat in her cheeks. 'I'm his assistant, yes.'

'Then where the hell is he? I had a meeting booked
with him in the conference room at ten-thirty. I got an
earlier flight back from the States to make sure I was
here on time, I'm jet-lagged, in dire need of a shower
and something to eat, and there's no sign of your boss
anywhere. Care to tell me where you think he is, Miss
McKenzie?'

Right now, what she actually *cared* to tell Mr High-
and-Mighty-I'm-so-much-better-than-you standing in
front of her was probably unprintable, but she was
equally angry with Derek. Why hadn't he briefed her on
the fact he had a ten-thirty appointment with this man,
whoever he was? She'd checked the diary thoroughly before she'd left last night, as she always did, and there had
been no meeting in the conference room at ten-thirty pen-
cilled in then. What the devil was he playing at?

Her heart sank at yet another painful reminder of her boss's slow and steady decline. Once a smart up-and-coming young architect, since his divorce Derek Holden had turned more and more to the bottle in search of comfort. In the past six months Morgen had seen him turn into a sad, shambling wreck of his former self. It was a good job that she was quick-witted and smart herself, because she had saved his bacon on more than one occasion—taking over work that was definitely not in the province of a mere personal assistant. She concluded that Derek must have known about the meeting for a while but had forgotten to tell her about it.

Now, as her fingers turned over the wide pages of the desk diary, hovering over the blank space next to ten-thirty, Morgen frowned down at it, rapidly scanning her brain for the best excuse for his absence she could possibly come up with. Sensing the man's irritation grow more acute as the seconds ticked by, she reflected that this handsome Goliath in front of her was going to take a heck of a lot of convincing.

'Unfortunately Derek has been taken ill,' she explained smoothly, assuring herself she wasn't too far off the mark. He usually didn't show up until around ten most days anyway, but because it was now almost eleven-fifteen she assumed he must be feeling even more the worse for wear than usual. He probably wouldn't show up today at all—which might be for the best, considering the glowering face before her.

'Really? Then why in hell's name didn't someone let me know?' The deep, resonant bellow almost made Morgen jump out of her skin. 'Why didn't *you* let me know, Miss McKenzie? Isn't that what you're paid to do?'

'If you'd care to tell me who you are, I might be able to—'

'Conall O'Brien. Obviously you weren't even aware that your boss and I had a meeting, were you? Care to explain why?'

Her head hurt at the relentless barrage of questions, but her pulse nearly careened to a halt like a car coming upon a sudden hairpin bend when he said his name. Conall O'Brien. The charismatic head of O'Brien and Stoughton Associates—premier architects with offices in London, Sydney and New York. Although Morgen had worked for the London office for just over a year now, she had never set eyes on the man himself. However, his awesome reputation preceded him.

It was well known that he took no prisoners and showed little leniency to anyone having personal problems—a fact that had been made abundantly clear to her already. He absolutely hated tardiness and expected one hundred and ten per cent from the people who worked for him. He mostly worked out of the New York office, and occasionally Sydney, but she had never known him to come to London in all that time—he had always sent a representative. How on earth could Derek have forgotten to brief her on something so important? His love for the bottle might have finally put both their jobs in jeopardy.

A single mother with a six-year-old daughter and a mortgage to pay, Morgen couldn't afford to lose her job right now. Her day had started badly, because she'd been up all night nursing Neesha's cold. Then falling asleep at her desk due to exhaustion—could this day get any worse? she wondered. While she was contemplating this, eyes the colour of a freezing Atlantic Ocean in a squall bored unmercifully into hers, and Morgen knew she had a long way to go to redeem herself in front of this man.

'I know this doesn't look good, but Mr Holden has been working terribly hard lately. Yesterday he definitely looked under the weather. I'm not surprised he isn't in today.'

'Never mind that. Why weren't you aware that we had a meeting? Dammit, it was arranged only last week. Presumably you and your boss do communicate?'

To Morgen's alarm he shrugged off his trench coat and threw it on a chair beside the window that reflected the impressive high-rise vista of the city of London. He was dressed from head to foot in bespoke tailoring that screamed quality and money. The suit was a deep dark blue with a very faint pinstripe, matched with a royal blue shirt and silk tie, and its wearer exuded the kind of power that mostly only those born to wealth and privilege could effortlessly carry off. Coupled with that watchful intelligence in those 'I'm not missing a damn thing' arctic blue eyes, and those intimidatingly broad shoulders, he clearly wasn't a man to be trifled with. Though right now Morgen wasn't trifling at all. She was fighting for her life in deadly earnest.

'Of course we communicate. Derek—Mr Holden obviously meant to tell me to put it in the diary, but because he was so busy he unfortunately forgot. I can assure you it's very unlike him, Mr O'Brien. Why don't I pour you a cup of coffee and maybe send out for some food, if you're hungry? And in the meantime I could ring Mr Holden at home and tell him you're here. He could jump in a taxi and be here in about twenty minutes or so, I'm sure.'

'From that comment I take it that he's not exactly at death's door, then?'

Feeling her face burn, Morgen dissembled. 'I'm afraid I don't have any details at present.'

'So go get the coffee, then get me Holden on the phone—I'll talk to him myself. Don't worry about food—I've got a lunch appointment at one, so it will keep.'

Pulling out a chair from the wall, he dropped down into it opposite Morgen's desk, his impressive frame all but dwarfing it. Yet she would swear there wasn't so much as an ounce of superfluous flesh on that awesome physique. Intensely aware of every single thing about the man, she didn't miss the yawn he swiftly suppressed or the faint look of weariness that briefly glimmered in those quick-witted blue eyes.

She couldn't help but be relieved when she escaped from the room into Derek's office, to pour some coffee from the percolator that was always kept on simmer. As far as Morgen was concerned the air around Conall O'Brien was far too rarefied for her liking, and she wondered how the people in his office coped with the man. When Conall said 'jump', did they all jump automatically? Probably…either that or risk being fired.

Crouching down in front of the cabinet where she kept the best crockery, only used when Derek was in conference with VIPs, Morgen cursed softly as several empty whisky bottles fell out onto the thick grey carpet and rolled towards her feet. As she quickly started to gather them up the door opened quietly behind her, and she found herself in the humiliating position of being caught red-handed.

'Very unlike your boss to "forget" our appointment, you say, Miss McKenzie?' His voice dripping with icy disdain, Conall fixed his unforgiving gaze on Morgen. 'I guess if I had a belly full of whisky I'd be inclined to forget my commitments as well…wouldn't you agree?'

Her startled green eyes widened as she glanced up at him, and her stomach turned decidedly queasy at the fact that poor Derek's unhappy drinking problem was no longer exclusively their little secret. 'If you'd—if you'd like to wait outside I'll just get rid of these and make your coffee.'

'Leave them.'

'It's all right. It will only take a minute, then I'll—'

'Leave the damn bottles, Miss McKenzie, and get that feckless boss of yours on the phone, pronto!'

Morgen's knees were shaking as she got to her feet. Her lips pursed, she turned away from the accusing glare of a pair of wintry blue eyes and went to reach for the phone on Derek's desk.

'Wait a minute.'

'What?'

'On second thoughts, right now I need a caffeine fix more urgently than I need to tell your dear Mr Holden his services are no longer required.'

Her heart sinking, Morgen replaced the phone shakily back in its cream-coloured rest. 'You don't mean that.'

'What?' A briefly amused quirk of perfectly sculpted lips brought the first glimpse of a smile, but Morgen steeled herself against falling into such a trap. He wasn't going to lure her into any sense of false security so easily. 'You don't believe I need a caffeine fix?'

'It's not that. I just—I mean, you can't fire Derek! He's a good man. Honestly…he'd do anything for anybody. His wife left him recently, and he hasn't coped with it very well. I've no doubt he'll turn things around, given the chance.'

'Spoken like a loyal and true assistant. Is that *all* you

do for your boss, Miss McKenzie? Help him in the office?'

The insinuation was so blatantly obvious that for a moment Morgen was dumbstruck. Then, with trembling hands, she drew the black lapels of her suit jacket together over her blouse and, with all the dignity she could muster, raised her gaze to look Mr High-and-Mighty O'Brien straight in the eye.

'I don't care for your crude implications, Mr O'Brien. If you knew Derek Holden then you'd know that he only had eyes for Nicky, his wife. And if you knew me then you'd also know that I make it an absolute rule never to get involved with anyone at work.'

'Never?' The brief smile suddenly became teasingly wider, revealing perfectly white teeth against his tan, and Morgen had to concentrate hard so that she could think.

Folding her arms across her chest, she deliberately didn't smile back. *How dared he? How bloody well dared he make casual sexual insinuations when she was in fear of losing her job as well as her boss?* But then she guessed that not many people would dare stand up to this man without fearing the consequences. Well, perhaps he'd met his match in her. Because, as much as she needed this job—and God only knew how much—she wasn't about to cower in a corner because this man had the power to intimidate.

'Absolutely never, Mr O'Brien. Now, if you'd care to wait in the outer office, I'll get you that coffee you're apparently so desperately in need of.'

For a long tension-filled moment, during which Morgen would swear the only thought in his mind was to give her the sack on the spot, Conall treated her to one of his hard, unrelenting stares, then surprisingly turned away to move towards the door.

'Strong and black, Miss McKenzie—no sugar. You don't mind if I use your office to do some work?'

'Go ahead.'

Feeling like a deflated balloon, she almost sagged against the desk when he'd gone. When she next saw Derek...she couldn't decide whether she'd read him the Riot Act or simply wring his neck.

Conall drew out a sheaf of papers from his briefcase and rubbed at the pain throbbing in his temple. If he didn't catch up with some sleep soon they'd have to carry him out of there on a stretcher. It wasn't because he was unaccustomed to a long working day, or even working seven days a week—it was all grist to the mill as far as he was concerned. That was how he'd built up the business when his father had retired to 'let his son take the reins'. But, having had non-stop meetings five days running and then two consecutive long-haul flights—one from California to New York, where he'd touched base at the office, then from New York on to London—his body needed sleep like a prisoner on Death Row needed to stay awake.

Taking another mouthful of the strong black coffee Morgen had brought him, he stopped reading the writing on the page in front of him and thought about the woman he'd just met. Where he lived they used the expression 'hot'. As far as her figure and her face went, Morgen McKenzie was on fire. Even though his rage at her boss's ineptitude, as well as finding her asleep at her desk, had almost made him lose it big time, his hormones wouldn't have been in prime working order if he hadn't reacted to the beautiful girl in front of him. And, God knows, he'd reacted.

When he'd discovered her on her knees in Holden's

office, trying to hide the blatant evidence of the man's drinking problem, it had taken just one dazzling glance from those big green eyes of hers to almost make him forget what he was there for. It hadn't helped matters either when the vee of her blouse had gaped a little, unwittingly giving him a very sexy glimpse of her gorgeous cleavage, white lace bra and all. He'd received a sexual charge so acute that for a moment his thoughts had been scrambled to the four corners of the earth.

Of course he couldn't help being angry that she'd been asleep at her desk. He had a reputation for being hard but fair to his employees, and could be generous to a fault to the people who deserved it, but he absolutely deplored slackers—workers who didn't pull their weight. One look at Morgen and he'd hazarded a guess that the lady had been burning the candle at both ends—no wonder she was tired! With looks like hers she doubtless had a queue of admirers going round the block—what reason would she have to stay home and mope when she could be out on the town every night? Never mind the effect it had on her performance at work. The thought made his blood boil. Who would blame him if he gave her her walking papers along with her boss?

Conall sighed and rubbed a hand round his beard-roughened jaw. Trouble was, Derek Holden had been a rising star amongst the young architects in the UK office. Up until recently Conall had only received the best reports. One of the main reasons for his visit—apart from appeasing his mother—was to find out what had been going wrong. Of course he wasn't about to reveal as much to the provocative Miss McKenzie. He decided he'd let her stew for a little while—keep her guessing as to whether she or her boss were about to lose their jobs. That at least ought to get some proper work out of her.

'Can I get you some more coffee?'

She breezed into the room, a flush on her pretty face that was immediately arresting and her dark hair floating loose from its fastening. Conall sensed straight away that she'd been up to something.

'Who were you phoning?' he asked smoothly, using the time to make another leisurely inventory of her face and figure. 'Could it be the hapless Mr Holden, by any chance?'

Guilt was written all over her face as plain as day, and Conall wondered if her feelings were always so transparent.

'If I'd spoken to Derek I would have told you,' she replied testily. 'If you must know I rang my mother—to let her know that I'd probably be home late.'

'You live with your mother?' Now she had really surprised him. Conall studied her features with renewed interest, momentarily mesmerised by her sexily shaped mouth with its highly desirable plump lower lip. He put down his coffee cup and made a discreet adjustment to his sitting position.

'She's staying with me at the moment because she hasn't been very well.'

Morgen hesitated to reveal that the real reason her mother was staying with her was that she was looking after Neesha, her daughter, who had been poorly these last few days. Her stomach tightened at the thought of her little girl suffering in any way, but she couldn't afford to take time off when Derek was absent from the office more often than he was in. Especially not now, when she had the big boss breathing down her neck, probably looking for any reason—however trivial—to sack her. She didn't want him automatically assuming, as so many employers did, that if she had a child she would be somehow less reliable or committed to her job. The truth of the matter was that she was even *more* reliable and committed to her job because she had responsibilities at home.

Frustration bit along her nerves. She wished he wouldn't look at her so closely, as if she was some sort of interesting foreign object beneath a microscope. Ever since that remark earlier, about what she did for Derek, she'd been feeling extremely self-conscious. If only he would go! Why was he hanging around in her office when he could surely hang around with the VIPs upstairs? Was he laying some sort of trap to catch poor Derek out?

'I'm sorry to hear that, but if you think I'm going to be more lenient with you because you've got troubles at home, then I'm afraid you're going to be disappointed, Miss McKenzie.'

Was he going to sack her? A wave of anger washed over her at the thought. It was so unfair! She hadn't had one day off since she'd started this job, and she stayed until at least six or six-thirty most nights. Just her luck to doze off at her desk and for him to walk in right at that moment! She'd even given up several Saturdays to accompany Derek to site meetings and take notes, but what would Mr Big-Shot know about that? No, he'd simply taken one look at her and assumed the worst. Well, she wasn't going to go down without a fight, that was for sure!

'Are you threatening me, Mr O'Brien?'

'I found you asleep at your desk, Miss McKenzie. In my book that's a sacking offence.'

His jaw was very square and very hard-looking, and right now Morgen wanted to punch it and knock him off his chair.

'And does the concept "innocent until proven guilty"

ring any bells with you?' She was shaking so hard that she was barely able to get the words out.

Conall leaned forward to lay his sheaf of papers on her desk, then leaned back again with his hands behind his head as if amused.

'What's to prove? There is no doubt in my mind that you were asleep when I walked into the room. Unlucky for you the last time I had my eyes tested I was assured I had twenty-twenty vision.'

'There was a perfectly good reason that I fell asleep—and it was for all of five minutes, if that!'

She heaved a breath that strained at the buttons on her blouse and Conall became transfixed by the sight. He wanted to ask her to have pity. It seemed the lady just had to take a breath and lust took the place of the cool professionalism he usually maintained. His gaze drifted back to her face and those flashing green eyes of hers. He had no intention of sacking her, but he wasn't averse to playing a little cat and mouse either.

'Okay. Convince me.'

He was just so smug and self-righteous sitting there that suddenly Morgen lost the urge to prove anything. Let him think what he damn well liked, for all she cared! There were other jobs besides this one. She'd just have to temp for a little while until she found something more permanent. Though the thought didn't hold much appeal, and she was genuinely upset at the idea of leaving Derek in the lurch. Particularly now, when he needed all the support he could get. Still...

'I've changed my mind.' Smoothing down her skirt with a trembling hand, she turned on her heel and stalked back into Derek's office with her head held high.

Stunned, Conall pushed himself to his feet, loosened

his tie and followed her. He found her pulling files from a tall mahogany cabinet and laying them out on the desk.

'I said convince me, Miss McKenzie.'

'Go to hell! And if that's a sacking offence too, then I've well and truly been given my marching orders, haven't I?'

'It would mean so little to you, losing your job?' Frowning, Conall watched her stalk to and fro from the cabinet, somehow deflated that he had pushed her too far. If that wasn't bad enough, there was a little niggle in the centre of his chest that told him he might just be wrong about Morgen McKenzie. That being the case, he didn't want to lose someone who might turn out to be a valuable employee.

'There you go again, making assumptions about situations you know nothing about!' She stopped her agitated stalking and dropped her hands to her hips. 'My job is very important to me, Mr O'Brien, and if you'd care to ask around in the office you'd more than likely find out that I do it well—at least, I haven't had any complaints so far. Unfortunately Derek isn't here right now to corroborate the fact. Perhaps when he does come in you can ask him.'

'And do you really believe his good opinion is honestly worth having?' Raising his eyebrow, Conall waited with interest for her answer.

'If you're referring to the bottles…' Morgen's eyes drifted towards the now closed cabinet and a tinge of pink highlighted her beautiful cheekbones. 'The fact that he's got a problem with drink doesn't make him a bad person, or a man whose opinion doesn't count. He's won awards for this company, Mr O'Brien, as I'm sure you must be aware. He's a talented architect with a bright future. Right now he needs help and support. He doesn't deserve to lose his job because his world suddenly fell apart when his wife walked out.'

'And what about what this firm deserves, hmm?' Rubbing at the smooth tanned skin between his brows, Conall frowned. 'We have our reputation to think of…clients who expect a first-class service. If that level of service starts to suffer because of individuals like Derek Holden, who can't cut it when their personal lives start to encroach on their work, then I'm sorry—but we're not in the business of extending patience indefinitely. If he can't get his act together pretty soon then there are plenty of other ambitious young architects waiting to fill his shoes.'

Several thoughts jumped into Morgen's head at once, but one inched ahead of all the rest. The man was ruthless…unbending. He didn't care if Derek was suffering the torments of hell. All Conall O'Brien cared about was that right now Derek wasn't 'cutting it'—ergo, he wasn't making any money for the firm. It would serve him right if she walked out right now in protest. Nobody was indispensable, that was true, but he was going to have a hell of a time making sense of things without her around to explain them. Especially when all the other secretaries were run off their feet as well. She was tempted to do it, too.

Seeing the conflict in her troubled green eyes, Conall feigned a look of boredom, wondering what she'd do if he called her bluff.

'So, Miss McKenzie…are you staying or going?'

'I won't let Derek down.' She was fidgeting with her hands, and her angry glance slid away from Conall's unflinching stare. Her emphatic statement made it quite clear that it was Derek she owed her allegiance to—not him or the firm.

He wanted to admire her loyalty—no matter how misplaced, in his opinion. After all, hadn't her boss let her down too, leaving her to face the music while he drowned his sorrows at home? But Conall found he couldn't. It irked him immensely that she insisted on trying to protect a man who clearly didn't deserve it.

'Good. Now that we've established that you don't want to make yourself unemployed, perhaps we can get some work done around here?'

The expression on Morgen's face told him she wanted to throw something at him. The fact only hardened his resolve to deal with the situation in his own inimitable way—the way that had turned his father's business into the successful firm it was today. Conall gestured at the unopened files on the desk. 'Are these current projects?' When she nodded mutely, he slipped behind the desk and sat down in the big leather chair that Derek Holden usually occupied. 'Bring me some more coffee and I'll take a look while I'm here.'

Biting back 'I'm not your servant,' Morgen swallowed her pride and reluctantly returned to the outer office to fetch his cup. As she poured coffee with a shaking hand, she couldn't help wondering for how long she and her boss would keep their jobs now that their dictatorial senior partner had made his ominous presence felt.

CHAPTER TWO

THE ringing of the phone on her desk made her jump. She snatched it up guiltily, wondering if Conall was straining an ear to keep tabs on her movements. Glancing at the door to Derek's office, and seeing it closed, she breathed a sigh of relief.

'Morgen McKenzie.'

'It's Derek.'

'For goodness' sake! Where are you?' Cupping the mouthpiece with her hand, she turned her head again, to make doubly sure the door to the other office was shut.

'I'm at home. Where do you think I bloody am?'

As Morgen had expected, he sounded irritable and hung-over. Her stomach knotted with deep apprehension.

'Do you know who you missed an appointment with this morning?'

'Don't play games with me, Morgen, I'm not in the mood. Whoever it was I'm sure it will keep. Thankfully, you always come up with the perfect excuse to explain my absences. That's what makes you such a priceless assistant.'

'And that's supposed to be a good quality? Lying?'

'What?'

She heard the chink of glass, then something heavy thud to the floor. Instinct and experience told her that he had already been drinking this morning and probably still was. If Conall caught so much a whiff of the fact they'd both be for the high jump.

'Your meeting was with Conall O'Brien, Derek. Does the name ring any bells?'

'Oh, sh—!'

'My sentiments exactly. However, that doesn't do either of us any good. He's still here in your office, waiting to see you. First impressions predispose me to believe that he's prepared to wait quite a while until you show up.' Though he had mentioned to Morgen that he had a one o'clock lunch appointment, she remembered. Glancing down at her watch, she saw that it was a little after twelve-thirty. Thank God the man would be leaving soon—but, more importantly, how soon would he be back?

'Have pity, Morgen! I'm in no fit state to deal with that man. I can't possible—possibly come in today. You'll have to tell him I'm ill or something.'

Gritting her teeth, Morgen glared at the phone. 'I've already told him that, Derek, but quite frankly I don't think he believed me.' Now wasn't the time to reveal that Conall had wandered into his office the very moment Derek's empty whisky bottles had rolled out onto the floor in front of him. If he knew that he'd been rumbled—by the head of the firm, no less—there was no telling what Derek might do in his present state of mind. 'You'll just have to try and come in. Make some coffee, then grab a quick shower. I'll order you a taxi and meet you downstairs in the lobby.'

He sighed noisily in response. 'I can't do it. I feel like death, if you must know. You're asking me to do the im-impossible.'

Damn Nicky Holden for leaving him in the lurch! But what was the use of blaming his wife? It was Derek's reaction to the whole sorry mess that was making things worse. Who would have thought that a successful, confident, bright young man who designed major projects worth millions of pounds would fall apart like a house of cards because his marriage hadn't worked out? Morgen could only wonder. It wasn't that she was unsympathetic. She had been through a similar scenario herself, and been five months pregnant to boot when her husband Simon had walked out. The difference being that she just hadn't had the option of falling apart. Not when she had a baby to take care of and a widowed mother who constantly looked to her for support.

Sighing now, she scraped her hand through her hair and completely dislodged the little tortoiseshell comb that held it in place. The dark silky strands of her shoulder-length hair escaped to slip round her face.

'There's only one thing for it, then. I'll come to you and help you sort yourself out. I'll be with you just as soon as I can order a cab. For God's sake, stay put—and, Derek…?'

'Yes, Morgen?'

'Don't drink any more. If you want to make yourself useful put the kettle on and have a bite to eat. Got that?'

At the other end of the phone the receiver clattered down without a reply.

Morgen was just grabbing her coat off the chrome coat tree when the door swung open and Conall strode back into the room. His sudden appearance put the fear of God into Morgen, and she hated the fact he could so easily intimidate her. His arms folded across that impressively wide chest of his, he eyed her consideringly, like a big cat about to play with a mouse. Damn, damn, damn! Wasn't she allowed any luck today? It seemed not.

'Going to lunch already, Miss McKenzie?'

'I've got an appointment. I'll only be about an hour, if that. I was just…I was just coming to tell you.'

'Were you, indeed?'

Was the man always so untrusting? Morgen huffed an exasperated breath and tried valiantly to meet his gaze. No easy undertaking when those cold blue eyes looked as if they would spear shards of ice into her body at any moment.

'I know you don't believe me, but I really have to be somewhere right now. I promise I won't be long, and if you need me to stay late tonight I'll be only too happy to do so.' It almost killed her to say it when she knew Neesha was probably pining for her. Her little girl loved her nana, but it was Morgen she wanted when she was feeling poorly. Still, she would do all she could right now to keep her job. She only prayed that Neesha would be feeling much better by the time she got home.

'Would you be going to meet your boss, by any chance?' Intently studying the suddenly surprised green eyes, Conall knew he had struck gold. Loyalty in general he admired—but subterfuge to dig her boss out of a hole? Well, that was a whole different ballgame in his book. He didn't know whether to be more furious with Morgen, for thinking she could pull the wool over his eyes, or the errant Derek, who had let himself slide from grace so ignominiously.

Worrying at her lip, Morgen swept back her hair with her hand. It drew Conall's appreciative male gaze to the luxurious glossiness of it.

'He's going to come into work. He just needs to freshen up a little and sort himself out.'

'And you're going to help him? What are you going to do? Hold his hand while he gets into the shower?' The very idea of this raven-haired temptress and a shower did things to Conall's libido that could be constituted as sexual torment.

Morgen didn't think it would do her case any good to confess that it wouldn't be the first time she'd gone to Derek's house with rescue in mind. She was practically as familiar with the layout of the once swish Westminster apartment, with its stunning Thameside view, as she was with her own small terraced house in Lambeth. Only the inside of Derek's once lovely home was no longer quite so lovely, due to neglect. Even his cleaner had quit, telling Morgen that she was tired of disposing of empty bottles of booze at every turn.

'Like I said before, he just needs a little bit of support through this difficult time. We can't just abandon him.'

'We?' Conall's eyebrows shot up to his hairline.

'The firm…me. Don't you want him to get better?'

She frowned, like a little girl who didn't understand some particular adult peculiarity, and something told Conall that she was too damn caring for her own good. However, it wasn't enough to make him restrain his temper. 'I'm running a business here, Miss McKenzie, not a care home.'

He saw her blanch. Did Derek Holden in his alcohol-ridden state know that his beautiful raven-haired assistant was championing his cause while he was away? Probably…no doubt the man was using that very fact to what he hoped would be great advantage.

'Don't bother calling a cab; I've got a car downstairs. I'm coming with you…to see if I can't help to talk some sense into him. Lead the way.'

'But what about your one o'clock meeting?'

'I've already postponed it. Now, let's go and discover what kind of condition your boss is in.'

*   *   *

Derek's already pallid face turned deathly white when he saw the visitor Morgen had brought with her. Stumbling back inside the wide hallway, with its once shiny parquet floor, he drove his hand through his dishevelled brown hair, desperate to regain some composure but failing miserably.

The air smelt old and stale, as if nobody had opened a window for a very long time. Morgen took one look at her boss and wished she had a magic wand so that she could put all that ailed him right in an instant. Turn back the clock to the time before Nicky had walked out on him, when he'd been a man who was very clearly steering his own ship, carving out a name for himself in what could be a highly competitive cut-throat business and acquitting himself with distinction.

'Hello, Derek. Why don't I make us all some coffee? Have you eaten?'

When he mumbled incoherently in reply Morgen slipped past him, reluctantly leaving him to deal with Conall alone. In the huge fitted kitchen, where there was every modern convenience known to man but not so much as one clear work surface to stand a cup on because dirty crockery was everywhere, Morgen rolled up her sleeves and got stuck into some of the mountain of washing up. She doubted there was a clean mug or cup in the whole place, never mind a clean percolator, and she couldn't make coffee without it. From experience she knew that Derek wouldn't give house-room to the instant stuff. At least, he wouldn't if he were sober…

Finding herself too interested in the now raised voices, Morgen turned on the hot tap to full flow to drown out the sound and grimly occupied herself with the task in hand. She knew instinctively it was little use praying that Conall would go easy on Derek—in terms of possibility that would be akin to expecting a boa constrictor to go easy on a mouse. Going easy on him would probably not get them very far, anyway. She'd tried the softly, softly approach herself, and Derek had merely laughed and told her that he definitely had his drinking under control and not to worry.

Five minutes later, sensing movement behind her, she turned to find Conall in the doorway minus his jacket and tie. He was a big man—strong and fit—and looked as if he could take on a whole army and emerge victorious. With his hair slightly disarrayed, and his hard jaw un-shaven, there was something dangerously compelling about him that couldn't be ignored, despite her silent vow that his good looks cut no ice with her.

'He's going in the shower. Can you have that coffee ready when he comes out?' His keen-eyed gaze moved curiously round the room as he spoke, and when he brought it back to Morgen he was shaking his head as if he couldn't quite believe the sight that confronted him.

'If we pay the guy enough to live in a place like this, why the hell doesn't he employ a cleaner?'

'He did.' Touching her cheek unknowingly, Morgen left a small trail of soapy suds on her skin. 'She walked out.'

'Why should that surprise me?'

About to turn away and return to see how Derek was faring, Conall found himself walking towards Morgen at the sink instead. Without a word, he reached down to gently stroke away the suds from her face. Up close, he saw that her green eyes were flecked with intriguing ha-zel lights and her dark lashes were long and luxurious—without the benefit of mascara, as far as he could detect. Her scent enveloped him for a moment—something warm and sensual, like a sunny day on the Cote D'Azur where he occasionally liked to holiday. His stomach muscles clenched iron-hard in response and a throb of heat went straight to his groin.

'You had some soap on your face.'

'Thanks.'

She turned away, clearly flustered. Smiling to himself, Conall walked back to the doorway. He liked the fact that he could ruffle her feathers. Truth to tell, he liked it a lot.

'How are you feeling now?'

Studying the pale, heavy-eyed features of the man before him, Conall wondered if there was really any point in dragging him back to the office for a meeting today. The hour in his office had given him enough time to brief himself on the current details of the big Docklands project Derek was presently in charge of, and he'd already rung the site manager and arranged a four o'clock meeting with the contractors and the client. He'd give Derek a day's grace to get his act together, and tomorrow morning first thing they'd have a meeting of their own, when Conall would lay out the options as he saw them before him.

Basically, the man had to agree to professional help or walk. There were already outrageous sums of money being wasted on this project through one discrepancy or another, as far as he could see, and Conall was damn sure his firm weren't going to help his client lose any more. Apart from that, they had an international reputation to protect—and protect it he would.

'Some more coffee would be good.' Feebly, Derek smiled and held out his mug.

Morgen relieved him of it and turned back into the kitchen. As she poured strong black coffee near enough to the brim her stomach rumbled, reminding her that she hadn't eaten a thing since dinner last night. Right on cue, her head started to throb. Too much coffee, not enough sleep and no food were not the best of combinations to aid health and vitality, she thought wryly, wondering when she'd find time to even eat the tuna sandwich her mother had put in her bag that morning. She prayed it would be soon, or she wouldn't be much help to anyone.

Poor Derek. 'Dreadful' didn't even begin to describe how he looked. 'Walking dead' was possibly more apt. Like a made-up extra in one of those old Hammer Horrors. There was no way he'd be any use in the office today; surely Conall could see that?

Hovering in the doorway while Derek manfully drank down his coffee, Morgen felt her nerves bounce badly every time her gaze connected with Conall O'Brien's. There was no doubt he was a formidable man, but he'd actually been much more lenient with Derek than she'd expected. She could have sworn she'd even glimpsed sympathy in his eyes every now and then as Derek had fumbled and stuttered an explanation as to how he had got himself into such a sorry state—but perhaps her senses had been deceiving her. Conall and sympathy just seemed to be the complete antithesis of each other. The man clearly judged having personal problems as some kind of major weakness.

Finally, glancing at his watch, he reached for his jacket on the back of the sofa and addressed Morgen directly. 'We'd better get back. I think Derek would be best served by sleeping off some of his excesses for the afternoon and coming into the office tomorrow instead. I've booked a four o'clock meeting with the contractors at Docklands, and you can come with me and provide back-up—fill me in on anything I'm not familiar with. You okay with that, Miss McKenzie?'

Normally Morgen wouldn't be fazed by such a prospect—she often accompanied Derek to site meetings—but this one was a biggie, and Derek had left the firm wide open to criticism by his absence and unwillingness to return phone calls. Consequently, as his assistant, Morgen had taken most of the flak. She'd been fending off irate telephone calls for days now, and she was certain it would become quickly evident to the gimlet-eyed senior partner of O'Brien and Stoughton Associates that a lot less had been accomplished on the project than he had a right to expect.

Suddenly a cuddle and a bedtime story with her lovely Neesha seemed even further away than it had this morning. Something told Morgen that this particular meeting would stretch well into the evening.

'That's fine with me, Mr O'Brien.'

'Leave the booze alone, Holden, and get an early night. If you want to keep your job, be in the office at nine tomorrow morning and we'll talk.'

Getting unsteadily to his feet, Derek threw a panic-stricken glance at Morgen as he followed them out into the hall to the front door. He was like a little lost boy, she thought, looking for her to save him. She turned away at the too familiar feeling, resenting it suddenly, but Conall didn't miss the brief warm smile of consolation she flashed back at the man.

He imagined what it would feel like to be on the receiving end of one of those gorgeous smiles himself. Pretty damn good, he reflected as she breezed past him out onto the stairwell, leaving a trail of her mesmerising scent. As she marched ahead of him back to the car his gaze locked onto those trim sexy calves in pale stockings and low heels and he knew he had a bad case of lust at first sight. The problem, as he saw it, was: what did he intend to do about it?

'I'm going back to my sister's place to get a shower and a shave. Can you hold the fort until I get back?'

Her backbone stiffening, Morgen flashed Conall an irritated glance. What did he think she'd been doing for the past six months while Derek slid further and further down the slippery slope of depression? Hiding in a cupboard?

'I'm sure I'll manage somehow.' Ripping her gaze away from his unwanted scrutiny, she wished she wasn't so acutely aware of the intimate confines of the luxurious car, with its cream leather upholstery and connotations of wealth and power.

'Why did his wife leave him?'

Conall's question took Morgen completely by surprise. Her hand was on the door handle beside her, but she withdrew it onto her lap, tucking her hair behind her ear as she spoke.

'He said she couldn't cope with his success. She was trying to forge her own career as a singer and felt that Derek didn't support her enough. They came from very different backgrounds, and in the end I suppose they just wanted different things. The differences just became too much to withstand—for Nicky anyway.'

Shrugging, she stared down at her own ringless hands, fighting off the unexpected sense of failure that suddenly descended on her out of nowhere. She didn't want to think about Simon, her ex-husband, but her last two sentences might have been describing their own disastrous union—brief though it had been. He had been an ex-pupil of Eton, one of the foremost public schools in the country, then gone on to medical school. When Morgen had met him he'd just been promoted to a registrar's job at Guy's Hospital, and his charm and total self-confidence had swept her away.

His parents were wealthy and his father, an eminent heart surgeon, had been knighted in the Queen's honours list. Morgen hadn't exactly received the red carpet treatment from his family, and straight from the off she'd known she wasn't good enough for their darling Simon. How could she be? She'd gone to a mixed comprehensive in South London, then trained as a secretary at a local technical college. Her father had been a bricklayer and her mother a school secretary. It went without saying that her family had hardly moved in the same illustrious circles the Vaughan-Smiths had frequented.

'These things happen.' Not taking his eyes from her, Conall wondered what she was thinking. 'He'll have to get over it soon. Especially if he wants to keep his job.'

'Derek isn't deliberately sabotaging his future. The man is in a lot of pain, for goodness' sake!'

Fielding off the frosty stare that accompanied Morgen's words, Conall knew she was probably thinking he was a hard bastard—someone who didn't give a damn about the people who worked for him as long as they helped the firm turn a profit. The truth was that he cared passionately about bringing out the best in people, and was only too happy to share the fruits of his own success with them when they did. However, that didn't mean he couldn't be tough when he had to be…ruthless, even.

As far as he could see Derek Holden had wallowed in his own self-pity long enough. If something were not done about that soon, it wouldn't just be the man's job that went down the pan, it would be his life. O'Brien and

Stoughton could easily hire another architect, but Derek couldn't be brought back from the dead.

'I'm well aware that the man needs help—professional help. In the meantime I'll be taking over things for a little while. You'll be working directly for me, Miss McKenzie. Think you can handle that?'

He couldn't help needling her, if only to see her react. Her captivating face instantly revealed her unhappiness. Her emotions were laid bare, and Conall realised it wasn't easy for her to don the civil mask of control that professionalism required. Not when in reality she was in turmoil. Inexplicably he felt himself warm to her in a way he hadn't warmed to a woman in a long time. And the prospect of being 'hands on' in the office while Derek took a necessary sabbatical—with Morgen as his assistant—suddenly appealed much more than it probably had a right to. As soon as he got back to his sister's flat in Highgate Conall would telephone the New York office and let them know he was extending his stay in the UK indefinitely.

'I can handle anything you care to throw at me, Mr O'Brien. Why don't you try me and see? Part of my secretarial course curriculum was how to deal with difficult people. In fact I specialised in it! See you back at the office.' And with that Morgen slipped out of the car, slamming the door behind her.

Conall laid his head back on the cream rest and mused that her hostility was probably a bonus. It would make it all the sweeter when she finally decided it was worth her while to be nice to him. Priding himself on knowing women as well as he did, and having personal experience that wealth and status in life were powerful aphrodisiacs—especially when it came to attraction—Conall didn't doubt that that would soon be the case…

CHAPTER THREE

AT THREE-THIRTY that afternoon Morgen made her way to the ladies' washroom to freshen up. Staring at her reflection in the bank of mirrors, she frowned at the soft bluish shadows beneath her eyes. She'd be lying to herself if she didn't acknowledge she looked just about as tired as she felt, but her spirits were lifted a little despite the tension of the morning because she'd heard from her mother that Neesha was more or less back to her old self today.

Reflecting on that fact now, she let her shoulders drop a little with relief. That meant that her daughter could go back to school tomorrow and her mother could go back home. Relationships were strained between them at the best of times, but none more so than when Morgen asked her to take care of Neesha for her when she was sick. Lorna McKenzie did not approve of women working full-time when their children were small. Truth to tell, Morgen might have shared the same conviction if Simon hadn't walked out on her less than a year into their marriage, drastically diminishing her options.

For a man who'd initially been over the moon to hear she was pregnant, he'd soon changed his tune as his wife's pregnancy had advanced. He dealt with sick people all the time, but he had professed he was unable to cope when Morgen was wretched with morning sickness. That, coupled with her lack of desire to socialise with his friends and never seeing eye-to-eye with his parents, had been good enough grounds for him to end the marriage as far as he was concerned. Besides, he really hadn't liked the idea of being 'tied down,' he'd explained as he was leaving. His career came first, and he really hadn't been sure whether fatherhood was for him after all. He was willing to help support her and the baby, but only until Morgen could return to work full time, at which time his future contributions would be for the child only.

'The child.' Simon still rarely referred to his daughter by her given name. She didn't see him from one month to the next anyway. By now Simon had made Specialist Registrar, and was on the fast track to becoming a consultant. He worked long hours and in his free time liked to play sport and socialise with his well-connected friends. As far as Neesha's grandparents went, Elizabeth and Terence Vaughan-Smith wanted nothing to do with their grandchild—they hadn't agreed with the marriage in the first place, so why should they acknowledge a child of that union?

Morgen stared hard into her own eyes and bit back the overwhelming desire to cry.

'Don't you dare, Morgen McKenzie!' she whispered harshly through gritted teeth, returning her pale rose lipstick to her make-up bag. 'You didn't cave in when the bastard walked out on you; you're not caving in now!' Her defences were low because she was tired, that was all. But her heart ached just the same for Neesha, because her father and his family had more or less rejected her.

Oh, well. Such was life. She wasn't the only one who'd had hard times and she certainly wouldn't be the last. Look at poor Derek. What would become of him if he were unable to turn his addiction around? At the thought of her boss she glanced down at her silver-linked wristwatch, noted the time, then grabbed up her bag from beside the sink.

Hell's bells! She didn't dare be late for Conall O'Brien—not when they had a four o'clock meeting to get to at Docklands. The man already thought she was lazy and incompetent—why make life even more difficult for herself by compounding that impression?

As she hurried back along the thickly carpeted corridor to her office, Morgen prayed she'd get there before Conall. She wasn't craving his approval, but neither was she courting his disapproval—and if he started to have a go at her, the mood she was in she'd probably tell him to stick his job where the sun didn't shine, and then where would she and Neesha be?

But luck, it seemed, wasn't on her side today. Standing by the window, gazing down at the London traffic through the slats in the blind, Conall turned as she entered, causing Morgen's heart to flutter like a moth flying too close to a flame. Newly showered and shaved, and wearing another impeccably tailored suit—this one a dark charcoal-grey matched with a pristine white shirt and burgundy-coloured tie—he looked like a man who meant business. He was clean-shaven, tanned and gorgeous, with piercing blue eyes that had her cornered the instant she set foot in the room, and it seemed that the world tilted more than a little when Morgen gazed back at him. The sensation made her strangely angry, not to mention defensive as hell.

'I haven't kept you waiting, have I? I literally just popped out to the washroom for a minute. Are you ready to go?'

'You look tired, Miss McKenzie. Are you sure you're up to this?'

Now he was casting aspersions on the way she looked, as well as her ability to do her job! Striding across the room, Morgen deliberately ignored him. Instead she gathered up the papers and plans on her desk, slid them into a large manila envelope, tucked it under her arm and walked back to the door.

'Shall we go, Mr O'Brien? It's already twenty to four. I just hope the traffic is in our favour.'

She'd tied back her hair, Conall noticed, almost as if trying to regain some lost control. The idea intrigued him, made him wonder if there were areas of her life where she willingly gave up the desire to stay in control. Like when she was in bed with a lover, for instance?

Although personally he preferred her beautiful hair left unconfined, however she wore it she would command attention—because Morgen McKenzie was not a woman who could pass unremarked. Her fitted suit accentuated a figure that veered more towards the voluptuous than the fashionably thin, but because she was tall as well—at least five eight, by his calculations—she could wear a black polythene sack and still look amazing. But he hadn't missed the dark circles beneath her lovely eyes either, and he was sure she was ready to kill him for noticing. Was his first impression of her right? Was she a party girl burning the candle at both ends most nights after work? And—more to the point—did she have a man in her life?

'That's what I like to see—enthusiasm for the job. It's going to be a long afternoon, by all accounts. I've already spoken with the client. Have you met Stephen Ritchie before?'

'We've only spoken on the phone,' Morgen replied, tension edging into her shoulders as she reflected on the irate telephone calls of the past week, not to mention the threats to sue the firm. All in all, Mr Ritchie did not sound like the kind of man she was eager to meet.

'Well, it's no exaggeration to say he's baying for our

blood—or Derek's blood, at least. We're going to have to jump through hoops to come out on top. Think we can save the day, Miss McKenzie?'

He paused in the doorway, crowding her with his impressive physique. His expression seemed to increase in intensity, causing a sudden outbreak of goosebumps beneath Morgen's clothes. Trouble was, the sexy fragrance of his cologne—along with the highly alluring and more subtle scent of the man himself—kept drifting in and out of her nostrils, making it hard to think. Unable to wrench her gaze away from his, Morgen sucked in a shaky breath. His seductive blue gaze had become a perilous ocean, and she was in mortal danger of becoming irrevocably lost at sea.

'I wish you would stop using my name as a means to taunt me, *Mr* O'Brien. I don't like being intimidated.'

'Is that what I'm doing? Intimidating you?' Frowning, Conall let his gaze sweep her features with genuine surprise.

Morgen couldn't find the words to answer him—not even a simple yes or no. Her senses were too besieged by his nearness.

'Would you prefer it if I called you Morgen?' he asked evenly, his voice dropping down a sensual octave or two.

Taken aback by his unexpected concern, she stepped hurriedly ahead of him into the corridor to cover her confusion. 'That is my given name.'

'Then Morgen it is.'

Easily falling into step beside her, Conall mused how well her name suited her. Morgan Le Fay sprang to mind—the legendary dark-haired enchantress in the tale of King Arthur. There was certainly something bewitching about her, that was for sure.

'Got everything we need, Morgen?' he asked conversationally, referring to the large manila envelope under her arm.

Her green eyes briefly met his. 'I've got everything you need, Mr O'Brien.'

Sweet heaven, he couldn't argue with that... 'Call me Conall,' he said brightly, just about getting the words out past the sudden aching dryness in his throat.

It was raining when they reached the site, where two new luxury apartment blocks were being erected. The rain had quickly turned the dry sand of the ground into a river of mud, and as Morgen donned the compulsory hard hat the site foreman gave her she wished she had had the foresight to bring some Wellington boots. Derek normally kept his in the boot of his car, and she had enough experience as his assistant to know that she should have done the same. As for Conall, he didn't seem to notice the fact that his black hand-made Italian shoes were quickly sinking into a quagmire of mud and sand.

After shaking hands with the stocky foreman, and introducing both himself and Morgen, he followed the man to the nearby planning office that had been erected to monitor progress on the site.

Inside, three other men—one of them suited—were seated round the long rectangular table. The smell of brewing coffee and cigarette smoke immediately enveloped Morgen's senses as they entered. All the men glanced at her with wary gazes, as though an alien had suddenly wandered in amongst them. Clearly some men still had old-fashioned views about women on a building site, she thought irritably, concluding it was about time they got over it.

'Miss McKenzie is my assistant and will be taking notes,' Conall explained, before pulling out a chair for her to sit down. 'Unfortunately Derek Holden is on sick leave, so I will be taking over the project until his return.'

From the first few minutes, as plans were laid out on the table and one of the men got up to pour the coffee into waiting mugs, it was evident who was in charge and why. Conall O'Brien's expertise in smoothing ruffled feathers and executing the necessary action to bring things back on course was a master-class in skill, diplomacy and people management bar none. Morgen saw and heard Stephen Ritchie's initially hostile reception to Conall melt like snow beneath a sun lamp.

Previously sluggish and tired, she straightened her back, sat up and listened in awe as the man finally had both the client and the contractors shaking hands and inviting him for drinks later on in the week.

Back in the car at ten to seven in the evening, Morgen swept a shaky hand through her hair and sighed as if she'd been let out of prison. The business of the day taken care of, she was more than a little anxious to get back to her little girl, and then for a hot bath and a stiff drink. Stealing a glance at the man beside her in the driver's seat, she was amazed that Conall O'Brien was showing no signs of fatigue or jet-lag whatsoever. Instead he was smiling as his big hands curved round the steering wheel, as if all was right with his world and everything in it.

'I thought that went well. How about you?'

The fact that he'd asked her opinion when it was glaringly obvious that things had gone more than well—he'd practically had them eating sugar out of his hand, for goodness' sake!—threw Morgen for a moment.

'I thought it was an exercise in damage limitation *par excellence*. Remind me to get you on my side when I'm next negotiating my car insurance.'

'Most people are driven by fear, Morgen. As soon as you come to realise that you're halfway there. You've got to get past your own ego to soothe theirs, and once you can do that—you're home free. You can get practically anything you want.'

She said nothing. The fact that he was willing to get past his own ego to soothe someone else's fears was enough food for thought for one day, she decided—even if there was an ulterior motive.

'I'm not rushing you, Mr O'Brien, but—'

'Conall.' There was mischief in his gaze, and it momentarily banished every coherent thought from her head.

'Fine. I don't want to rush you, but I'd really like to get home if we're finished for the day now. If you could drop me off back at the office I'll pick up my car and go.'

'Going out somewhere tonight?' he asked, expertly steering the big car smoothly away from the kerb.

'No.' Her answer was accompanied by a loud sigh. 'Definitely not. All I want to do right now is cuddle up on the sofa with my favourite person and relax in front of the TV.'

Her *favourite* person? Jealousy sliced through Conall's gut like a knife heated over a red-hot blaze. So there was a man in her life after all? He'd been stupid to hope there wasn't.

It was because he hadn't been in a relationship for a while, he reflected moodily as he drove through London's crawling traffic. A man had needs, and the delicious Miss McKenzie was a provocative reminder that his weren't being met. There was something singular about her that completely tantalised him. Hooked him up and reeled him in. Something in that slightly aloof façade of hers which could just as suddenly reveal her anxieties as candidly as a child's that made him want to get to know her better. Okay, so he badly wanted to get her into bed too. It was just his bad luck that she was already spoken for.

'What about you?'

'Excuse me?' Stealing a glance, he saw that she seemed to be waiting for him to speak.

'Have you any plans for this evening?'

Yeah. After he'd popped one of his sister Teresa's home-cooked meals in the microwave to heat he intended pouring himself a large glass of wine, then catching up with everything that had been happening in the New York office in his absence.

Unfortunately he did not have a *favourite* person to cuddle up to on the couch and watch TV with. It was just a shame that Teresa had been called away on business just before he'd caught his flight to Heathrow and would be gone indefinitely. She'd left her keys with a neighbour for him, but right now he could do with some company. He supposed after his transatlantic phone call he could ring his mother and speak to her, but he really didn't feel like listening to one of her lectures telling him it was high time he came back home to England for good.

'I'll probably be working.'

Shrugging, Conall made the necessary right turn, then reached out to switch on the radio. As a beautifully articulated voice announced the seven o'clock news from the BBC, he couldn't deny he was suddenly ridiculously glad to be home again—even if he was staying at his sister's and not a home of his own. There were definitely *some* things about the mother country that he missed.

'Mummy, why did Nana make you angry?' Her brown eyes pensive, the little girl with bobbed dark hair slid into bed and waited anxiously for an answer.

Morgen bitterly regretted that she'd given way to temper where her mother was concerned. But all she'd needed after a day fraught with tension—because of the arrival of Conall O'Brien, the sorry state they'd found her boss in and the anxiety of the site meeting—was for Lorna McKenzie to verbally demolish her as soon as she walked through the door.

Fingering the vee of her blouse, Morgen reached out to drop a tender kiss on Neesha's pink cheek, happy beyond measure that the child appeared to be so much better than she had been for the past few days.

'Nana and me just had a little difference of opinion, sweetheart. Sometimes it's hard for her to understand that I need to go out to work to support us both. But if there was any other way I could arrange things differently, believe me, I would.'

'Nana thinks you drove Daddy away because you were too stubborn. She thinks if you were nicer to him he would have stayed.' Neesha was biting her lip, and her expression was all eyes.

Feeling as if she had a lead weight in her stomach, Morgen clasped her daughter's small plump hand in her own and forced a smile.

'Nana had no right saying such a thing to you, honey. She doesn't want to accept that your daddy was scared about being a father. She thinks there must have been something I could have done to make him stay.'

No matter how 'nice' she might have been to Simon, he wouldn't have stayed. She knew that for a fact. Now there was a lump in her throat too. Not because she pined for him, but because she could see the confusion on her child's face. Why had her daddy abandoned her? How was a child supposed to understand that? Oh, how could her mother have been so selfish and stupid to say such things to her?

'Some people just aren't cut out to be parents, darling. It's a hard fact of life, but true, I'm afraid.'

'Then why did you and Daddy have me?'

'We made you because we wanted a baby—even if Daddy got scared later on and couldn't stay. And when I held you in my arms that very first time I thought you were the most beautiful, most perfect, most amazing little person that I'd ever seen in all my life, and I loved you with all my heart and always will.'

Clutching the child to her breast, Morgen breathed in the fresh clean smell of her hair, the impossibly soft black silky strands tickling her nose while the heat and softness of the sweet little body pressed fiercely against her own.

'I love you too, Mummy. You're the best mummy in the whole world *and* the prettiest. When I grow up I want to look just like you!'

Gently tucking her back down into her bed, with its quilted pink counterpane, Morgen smiled. 'You're good for my morale, you know that?'

'What's that?'

'Morale means your confidence—the way you think about yourself. You make me feel good when you say such sweet things to me. That's what I mean.'

'Good. I want you to feel good. I hate it when Nana makes you sad. I'll say goodnight now, Mummy, I'm feeling rather tired.'

'Okay, gorgeous. You snuggle down now, in your cosy bed, and I'll see you in the morning. You don't mind going back to school tomorrow?'

'I'm looking forward to it. I miss my friends.'

'I'm sure they've missed you too, poppet. Goodnight, angel, God bless.'

Back in the living room, Morgen stooped to pick up a purple stuffed elephant and an anatomically unlikely Barbie doll from the carpet, along with two dog-eared storybooks that were Neesha's favourites. Straightening the soft velvet cushions on the couch, she flopped down wearily, at the same time reaching for the remote and flicking on the television.

The choice of viewing was pretty dismal. Between a documentary on car crime, an awful soap whose soundtrack instantly depressed, football and one of those mindless reality TV programmes where members of the public were only too eager to humiliate themselves in front of the viewing masses, there was nothing to remotely tempt her. Pushing herself to her feet again, Morgen rifled through the bottom drawer beneath the television for a video.

When her hand settled on a much-loved romantic comedy, she knew that if the trials and tribulations of the perfect couple onscreen couldn't capture her attention then nothing would. Slipping the film into the VCR, then making a quick detour into the kitchen for a bag of crisps and some cheese, Morgen tucked her feet beneath her on the couch and settled back to enjoy the film.

When ten minutes had passed, and she realised she'd barely registered any of the action unfolding before her because her mind was unwittingly preoccupied with Conall O'Brien, she frowned deeply, then turned up the volume on the film to drive any further troublesome thoughts away. There was nothing about him she liked, she decided. Just because he was too handsome for his own good and was impressive under fire didn't mean that she was going to join his fan club. Along with his assets he was autocratic and domineering, and clearly possessed of a heart made of stone or something equally unbreakable. Thank God he was in the UK on a purely temporary basis, as far as she knew, and as soon as either Derek was back or they found a suitable replacement, Conall O'Brien would be back on a plane to America.

'Amen to that,' she said aloud, munching a handful of crisps. But even the impeccable credentials of the gorgeous hero onscreen, endearingly pleading his case to the equally gorgeous but wary heroine, for once didn't have the power to distract her from thoughts of the man she was certain she disliked intensely.

'Get those letters done and on my desk for signature in an hour, Miss McKenzie.'

Morgen's gaze moved from the stack of paper Conall had dropped onto her desk up to his broad shoulders in yet another classy suit as he strode back into Derek's office and slammed the door. She shook her head from side to side and grimaced.

'Whatever happened to "Would you prefer it if I called you Morgen"?' she queried beneath her breath.

Obviously he'd had a change of heart overnight. Perhaps he'd worked too hard and too long and jet-lag had finally caught up with him? Hah! The man didn't need an excuse to be ill-mannered. She'd bet her last penny it came naturally to him.

'Enough, already!'

Irritated beyond belief at the way he was getting to her, Morgen sifted through the impossibly untidy writing on the stacked pages before her, automatically prioritising them in order of importance. Twenty-four letters, some running to at least two pages apiece—was he trying to break some kind of record?—were not going to get typed up in an hour, no matter if her fingers were on fire. That said, she liked a challenge. Slipping off the black jacket she wore over a sleeveless pink top, she settled herself more comfortably in her seat, then swivelled round at the curved desk to face the computer at the other end.

Okay, so Conall hadn't imagined it—this intense, completely incomprehensible instant attraction to Derek Holden's raven-haired assistant. Just now, when he'd dropped those letters onto her desk and seen that voluptuous body of hers lovingly filling out a little black suit that, hard as it might try, did nothing to conceal those sexy curves, the wildly inappropriate desire that had stabbed through his body had completely staggered him. He'd had to retreat quickly to recover himself.

Now he stared out of the window at the familiar dome of St Paul's cathedral and completely missed the view. Last night when he'd been unable to get to sleep he'd naturally blamed the jet-lag. But if he was absolutely honest sleep had eluded him because he'd been plagued by erotic thoughts about Morgen McKenzie that had simply refused to go away.

'Damn!'

Curse words came easier than explanations right now. He had a lot to do today too. The phone hadn't stopped ringing since he'd set foot in the office at eight. News of his arrival had travelled fast, and the world and his wife wanted a piece of him just now…and that included his mother. He'd promised faithfully to drop by tonight for dinner, but already he was regretting it. He wouldn't be able to escape her reprimands about staying away for so long, and neither would he be able to avoid the usual unwanted references to him and his father.

Scribbling a reminder on a pad to get Morgen to send some flowers to his mother's address in Marylebone, Conall pulled open the door and decided there was no time like the present. She was seated at the computer, her slim straight back towards him, so Conall swung round to the front, where she could see him.

'A dozen long-stemmed yellow roses to that address, please. By lunchtime, if you can.'

'Any message?' Regarding him coolly above her computer screen, nonetheless Morgen felt her body grow uncomfortably hot beneath his sweeping blue glance.

'Sorry, can't make tonight after all. Ring you soon. Love, Conall.'

Glancing at the name and address on the sheet of paper he'd handed her, Morgen moved her head gently in a semi-nod. Victoria Kendall. Was she a girlfriend, fiancée, significant other? For the first time she considered the possibility of him being married. The thought elicited strangely mixed feelings, but right this minute she refused to delve too deeply as to why. Even if she had been remotely attracted to him—and she most definitely wasn't—Conall O'Brien was as way out of her league as Simon had been, even more so, perhaps. And look how that liaison had ended.

'I'll get onto it right away, Mr O'Brien.'

'Good. By the way, I trust you had a pleasant evening with your "favourite" person?'

For a moment Morgen didn't have a clue what he meant. Then she remembered what she'd said in the car last night, and her brow knitted in confusion at the suggestion of anger in his tone.

'I did, thanks.'

'I imagine a woman like you has a lot of *favourite* people?'

What the hell was that supposed to mean? Tossing her head, Morgen strove to keep an even tone. 'If you're implying something not quite complimentary, then I'd be pleased if you kept your thoughts to yourself. If you don't mind.'

'Why so secretive? Who is this *favourite* person of yours you clearly don't want to discuss?'

A muscle throbbed at the side of Conall's temple as he studied her, revealing that despite the controlled, polished, suave appearance he liked to project he was perhaps not at present as in control as he liked. Morgen wondered at that.

'I'm not trying to be secretive, for goodness' sake! And even if I were, aren't I allowed a private life?'

'Without a doubt.' Conall's response was clipped. 'I was merely expressing an interest. Aren't I ''allowed'' to do that?'

Her whole body tensing beneath his dogged determination to somehow extract the truth out of her, Morgen sighed irritably. Perhaps if she told him she'd spent the evening alone with her daughter that would be an end to his interrogation once and for all?

'The person I spent the night with is Nee—'

'Morning, all. Got any coffee going, Morgen? I'm going to need it.'

They both glanced round at the slightly rumpled figure of Derek Holden as he came ambling through the door, and it was all Conall could do not to curse his timing out loud.

CHAPTER FOUR

THE door swung open. After nearly two hours ensconced in his office, Derek preceded Conall out through the door, his slightly bewildered expression reminding Morgen of a prisoner suddenly released from confinement after a long period and wondering what exactly he was supposed to do with himself. Scratching his head, he gave her a lop-sided schoolboy grin. That grin concealed a multitude of torment, she didn't doubt. It squeezed Morgen's heart and she smiled back unreservedly.

'Well, Morgen, it looks like you've got yourself a new boss for the next six weeks. It seems I'm to take an enforced sabbatical—get myself straightened out. Think you can cope without me?'

Listening to his comments, Conall had to refrain from rolling his eyes. As far as he could glean Morgen had been holding the fort for several weeks now, while Derek showed up sporadically at best. Considering the pressure she must have been under to conceal her boss's 'little problem' as far as she could, as well as tackling the considerable workload, he had to admit a grudging admiration for her being able to pull it off. It was only in the past couple of weeks that it had really come to the attention of the associates upstairs, and then only because Stephen Ritchie had personally been on the phone to them about all the times Derek had let them down by not showing up on site. Alarm bells had started ringing and investigations had been made.

'You just get yourself better soon. Eat well and get

some rest,' Morgen advised. 'We'll manage here just fine.'

Realising that she had included Conall in that statement, she flushed with embarrassment. She knew that yesterday he'd mentioned he would be taking things over for a while, but that could mean just until he found someone else to step in for Derek. It didn't mean the man himself would be staying around indefinitely. At least, she hoped not. Her gaze slid away from both men as she deliberately returned her attention to the screen in front of her.

Conall accompanied Derek to the door, and after a final few words bade him goodbye. When he turned back to survey Morgen behind her desk he popped open the buttons of his suit jacket and pulled the knot of his tie away from his collar. Stopping to pour a cup of water from the cooler, he took a long, thirsty draught, then jettisoned the polystyrene cup expertly into the bin. Beneath his outwardly calm exterior he was secretly stewing on that last remark of Morgen's just before Derek showed up and interrupted them. 'The person I spent the *night* with,' she'd said. Right now he hardly trusted himself to speak to her, he was so irrationally angry.

'How are you getting along with those letters?' he asked.

'Fine. You haven't just left him to his own devices, have you?' Morgen demanded anxiously. She parried the flash of irritation in those perfectly blue eyes and stared right back at him to show she wasn't going to back down.

'Does that maternal streak of yours come out for every man, Miss McKenzie? Or is that particular trait reserved purely for the Derek Holdens of this world?'

'You're deliberately misinterpreting me—but then why should that surprise me? For your information, I'm not

mothering Derek at all. I'm simply acting out of concern
for a man who has been very good to me as a boss. He
may have had his own troubles to deal with, but he's
always treated me well and with respect. Which is more
than I can say for some of the men I've worked for!'

Conall flushed slightly beneath his tan at the barely
disguised reprimand. Did she think he didn't treat her
well? That stung. As for Derek…well, clearly Morgen
thought the man some kind of plaster saint! The throb of
jealousy presently zinging its way through his system
wasn't pretty.

'I'm sorry to hear that.'

He was about as sorry as an elephant who'd trod on
an ant, Morgen decided. 'Perhaps when it comes to treating staff decently you couldn't go far wrong if you took
a leaf out of Derek's book.'

In a pig's eye, Conall reflected with heat. But part of
him couldn't deny that he felt irritatingly guilty at her
reprimand. He'd always thought of himself as fair, but
firm—could he help it if the woman seemed to rub him
up the wrong way? He winced at his own poorly chosen
analogy. Still, it wouldn't do to let her imagine he was
party to any such weakness as guilt.

'It'll be a cold day in hell before I take a leaf out of
the book of a man who lets a woman leaving him reduce
him to a drunken, shambolic wreck!' he ground out
harshly. 'The man should have a bit more self-respect.'

Feeling all the colour drain out of her face, her fingers
gripping the desk, Morgen wondered how she would restrain herself from walking out there and then. But just
because Conall was clearly disparaging of a man like
Derek, who had suffered emotionally after his wife's
abandonment of him, it didn't mean that Morgen should
take his comments personally and resign. She might not

like what Conall had said, but from now on she would apply a much cooler head to the situation, and somehow remain aloof from the feelings of rage the man engendered inside her.

But, just the same, she'd be damned if she'd let him have the last word.

'You're so sure of yourself, aren't you?' Her green eyes sparkling with fury, she gripped the desk even tighter. 'You've probably never had a woman you cared for walk out on you. Beggar or king, it hurts, you know…to be abandoned by someone you love. Perhaps when it does eventually happen to you you might have a little bit more compassion for the rest of the human race!'

'Not likely, Miss McKenzie. I wouldn't let a woman get close enough to hurt me like that…though I'm not averse to getting close in other ways…'

Although his gaze never so much as wavered from her face Morgen received the disturbing impression that his contemplation of her was definitely bordering on the X-rated. Squirming in her seat, she wondered how he'd react if she told him that if he continued his inappropriate comments she'd report him for harassment. But even as the thought occurred she knew she would do no such thing. Who would take any notice of her when he was the boss?

But even as she thought that Morgen knew she couldn't lie to herself. When Conall O'Brien levelled his smoky looks at her, like him or not, the sensual nature that she had long buried since Simon walked out actually revelled in the attention, God help her. And now she was faced with the possibility of working for this man for the next six weeks!

Not wanting to fight any more, she swallowed down

her uneasiness and decided to make another attempt at reaching her implacable new boss on Derek's behalf.

'If you just leave Derek to his own devices he'll simply drink himself to death and that will be that! Don't you recognise the signs? The man thinks he's got nothing to lose since Nicky walked out. He's not thinking straight. How could he be? Couldn't you find it in your heart to help him in some way?' She hesitated to say *if you have one*…

'I hate to see you stress yourself out over this, Morgen. Confidentially, Derek's been booked into a very expensive and very exclusive drying-out clinic in the country, paid for by the firm. He'll have his every need catered for—except, of course, his need for alcohol. I've also arranged to receive weekly reports as to how he's faring. That put your mind at rest?'

Linking her hands together on the desk in front of her, Morgen exhaled a slow, difficult breath. All along he'd arranged treatment for Derek, and yet he'd let her rant on as if the last thing she could expect was for a man like Conall to help him. 'If you want to know the truth,' she admitted quietly, 'it does. I've had sleepless nights, worrying about what might happen to him.'

'And now your fears are hopefully laid to rest. He'll be in good hands.'

His reply was terse, dismissive. What could she expect when she'd been so outspoken in Derek's defence? Rude, really. She certainly hadn't pulled her punches. Reaching the door of Derek's office, Conall turned back at the last moment to glance thoughtfully her way.

'You should have talked to someone about your concerns for his welfare. That's what we have a human resources advisor for.'

'What, and have his dirty laundry aired all around the

office?' In spite of her vow to keep a cool head, she twisted her mouth scathingly. 'I don't know what it's like in the New York office, but here the gossips would have had a field-day. It's a shame, but people are only too eager to make their minds up about someone without knowing all the facts. Guilty until proven innocent. They would have had poor Derek hung, drawn and quartered before he had time to blink. Never mind his reasons for turning to drink in the first place. The man was in immense emotional pain. Right now they probably think you've given him the sack. By lunchtime the news will be all over the building.'

She was right, of course. He should have thought of it himself, Conall admitted silently. Hadn't he behaved in a similar fashion when he had had Morgen 'guilty as charged,' having discovered her asleep at her desk, without even knowing the first thing about her? It pained him to think that she had such a poor opinion of both him and her colleagues, despite the fact that he personally believed a lot of Derek Holden's emotional pain was self-inflicted and therefore didn't warrant such concern from her.

'Perhaps we ought to arrange some kind of informal meeting—make it official that Derek is on sick leave but expected to return in a few weeks' time? If it comes from me that ought to put a stop to any further speculation about him possibly losing his job.'

Directing the mouse on her computer pad to 'print,' Morgen inclined her head in immediate agreement. 'I could organise something for four o'clock this afternoon in the communal staffroom. Would that be okay?'

'I'll leave it in your capable hands. By the way, can you also organise me some lunch?' Conall's features relaxed into an unexpected smile. 'I'm going to be making a start on clearing some of Mr Holden's backlog. A sandwich at my desk will suffice. Something with chicken will do fine. Thanks.'

Morgen bet he could be almost charming when he tried, if that 'knock your socks off at twenty paces' smile of his was any indication. But she didn't want to be charmed by him, did she? His superior, arrogant manner she could handle, but his charm was another thing entirely…

Morgen sneezed, then sneezed again. As she slammed the driver's door shut a wave of heat descended, making her suddenly dizzy.

'Damn, damn, damn!' Shaking her head, she silently cursed the fates for giving her Neesha's cold. It really was the very last thing she needed, today of all days, when Conall was chairing a board meeting in the VIP suite and she was supposed to be taking notes. It was warm in there at the best of times, and if she got any hotter than she was at this moment it would be frankly unbearable.

Leaving the underground car park and making her way out onto the main road opposite the offices of O'Brien and Stoughton Associates, she had stepped off the pavement to get to the other side when suddenly a car whooshed by, practically taking the polish off her fingernails. At the same time a steely hand clamped her arm to yank her none too gently back onto the pavement. Before Morgen could recover herself Conall jerked her round to face him, jaw clenched and steely blue gaze swirling with anger.

'Have you got a death wish or something? Why the hell didn't you look where you were going?'

His heart was still beating much too fast. He hadn't

been able to believe it when he'd suddenly spotted Morgen, stepping out into the busy main road with a car bearing down on her at around thirty miles an hour. Seeing it swerve at the last minute to avoid her, he'd had to sprint to pull her back before the car that came after mowed her down. Now she was staring at him, her cheeks flushed and her pretty green eyes watery and confused.

Oh, Lord! She wasn't going to cry, was she? Conall prided himself on being as tough as the next strong, red-blooded male, but to be honest he was a sucker for weeping women, sick children and hurt animals. Frankly, all three were capable of hitting him where it hurt.

'Hey.' His voice turning gruff, he drew his knuckles gently down her cheek. A single tear gathered at the corner of one eye and slid down her flushed skin. 'I didn't mean to frighten you.'

Feeling as if there wasn't enough air to breathe, Morgen dug into her bag for a tissue, her insides quaking—more because Conall had touched her than because of her dramatic near-miss. Apart from realising that she had almost got herself killed, she was scared and confused that one man's touch could disorientate her so.

The roar of the traffic all but drowned out her shaky reply. 'You didn't frighten me. I was distracted for a moment, that's all. I should have been paying more attention to what I was doing. Thanks for coming to my rescue.' The thought occurred that if he hadn't her little daughter might well be motherless by now. That sparked off another tear, then another, until she was biting her lip to try and keep them at bay.

'Come on, let's go and get some coffee and talk a while.'

Slipping his hand beneath her elbow, Conall guided

her into a small Italian coffee bar just a little way down the road. Meanwhile Morgen was dabbing a little desperately at her tears—hardly able to believe that she was disgracing herself so badly, and in front of the one person she couldn't afford to show vulnerability to. He already had the opinion she was a shirker and not up to the job— now he would think she was a complete flake too.

A few minutes later, her senses assailed by the steamy fragrant aroma of coffee and newly baked rolls, Morgen sat facing Conall. His large frame dwarfed the chair, as usual, and his concentration was focused one hundred per cent on her—despite the steady stream of office workers dropping in for their early-morning refreshment. Her hand shook a little as she raised the creamy café latte to her lips, and the big man opposite frowned.

'Now, what's brought all this on? Maybe I can help?'

He really wanted to, Conall realised with an upsurge of longing. The distinct impression had been growing on him over the past few days that Morgen mostly went it alone, helping others without question and consequently neglecting herself. Just yesterday he'd wandered in on her comforting a distraught junior secretary whom he'd later found out had boyfriend trouble. He wondered if the 'favourite' person she had mentioned—Neil, or whatever his name was—really gave her enough support.

Then the thought of her boyfriend made him clench his jaw in irritation because, dammit, as far as Conall was concerned that was an obstacle he really didn't want to have to surmount.

'I'm fine, honestly. I've just picked up a cold and I haven't been sleeping very well.' Her glance was nervous and slid quickly away to avert further close examination.

Conall looked down into his coffee, then back again into her wary green eyes. 'I don't buy that as the only reason you're upset. What's been worrying you, Morgen? If it's anything to do with work I'm probably the best person you can talk to. The people who work for me are this firm's greatest asset. Therefore their wellbeing is my concern too.'

Put like that, his explanation sounded more than reasonable...seductive, even. But Morgen knew she couldn't confide in Conall. Apart from being only too aware that he was the owner and senior partner of the firm she worked for, she was already acquainted with the fact that he despised weakness of any kind. And, when it came right down to it, why would a man like him want to bother with an ordinary little secretary like her anyway? She'd already had one humiliating experience with Simon, and knew that huge differences in money and status could be a problem in relationships. She certainly didn't want to set herself up for a similar rejection again.

'I thought you didn't approve of people's personal problems encroaching on their work, Mr O'Brien?'

'Conall,' he said irritably, raking his fingers through his hair, then suffered immediate remorse because he had been taunting her with 'Miss McKenzie' from the beginning.

Had he done it subconsciously, in an attempt to put up a barrier between Morgen and himself? To keep their relationship strictly professional and somehow curtail the violent attraction that coursed through his veins every time he looked at her? He generally made it a strict rule that he didn't get involved with women at work. Those kinds of complications could and frequently did get messy, in his experience.

'You don't have a very high opinion of me, do you?' he added.

'You do what you have to do, I suppose. It doesn't

mean I have to like it.' Shrugging one shoulder, Morgen took refuge behind her coffee cup.

'You don't think I care about the people who work for me?'

She coloured. 'I didn't say that.'

'But you don't think I'm particularly sympathetic?'

Feeling as if she'd just blundered into a hedge of stinging nettles, Morgen wished she hadn't started this conversation. 'Your reputation precedes you, Mr O'Br—'

His brows drew together in an irritable scowl. 'If you call me that again, I'll fire you.'

Her heart thumped heavily.

'Like I said before, I'm running a business...' The rest was left unsaid. Conall couldn't understand why her comment had suddenly made him so uncomfortable. Had he become too hard-nosed for his own good? He was a success, wasn't he? His firm was a success. And he genuinely believed people liked working for him. So why should Morgen McKenzie's good opinion of him matter so much?

'I know that can't be easy.' Mentally fielding another wave of heat, Morgen cautiously considered him from beneath her lashes. 'But we're all human, you know? And life isn't a straight road with simple answers. Like I said before, I'm sure Derek didn't deliberately sabotage his career by turning to drink.'

'But we're not talking about Derek right now.' He rubbed his hand round the back of his shirt collar, then leant back in his chair and sighed. 'I'm sorry you don't feel that you can trust me enough to tell me what's bothering you. Perhaps we should talk about that? Not now—' He took a brief glance at his watch '—but as soon as we can arrange a little time together.'

The whole idea filled Morgen with intense trepidation.

It was testing enough having to work with this man, never mind arranging 'a little time together' to talk about why she felt she couldn't trust him.

'There's really no need. And, anyway, I've just got a cold. Nothing in particular is bothering me right now…' *Except you.* 'I'll be fine in a minute or two.' With an apologetic little shrug, she took another sip of the delicious coffee, feeling slightly calmer now, even though her skin still prickled with heat.

'Perhaps you ought to go straight home after the board meeting? I'll drive you myself.'

'No!'

The vehemence with which she voiced her reply made Conall's brows draw suspiciously together. Damn it all, the woman looked frightened. What was she trying to hide? A no-good feckless boyfriend who was unemployed, perhaps? Was that why Morgen looked so tired? Because she was supporting a man who relied on her to keep him? Anger briefly seared his gut, then he scolded himself for jumping to conclusions, making assumptions without knowing the facts—something Morgen had already had good reason to accuse him of. He suddenly saw there was ample reason for her not to trust him, and it was seriously beginning to get to him.

She didn't want him to drive her home. She didn't want him to see the small rundown street in which her poky two-bedroomed terraced house was situated. Not that she was ashamed of it—not when she had spent years lovingly turning it into a cosy, inviting little home for herself and Neesha. But it was surely way down the desirability league from what a man like Conall was used to. And if she so much as saw embarrassment or pity in his eyes he'd have her notice on his desk quicker than he could say Savile Row.

'I'll be fine to see out the day, then I'll drive myself home. Thanks all the same.'

Sensing it was futile to argue, Conall drank his coffee down in one long draught, then pushed to his feet. 'We ought to be getting back. I've got a full schedule today. Feeling any better now?'

'Much,' Morgen lied, her legs decidedly shaky as she followed him out through the door and into the street.

It was a long meeting—far longer than Conall would have liked. It seemed his fellow associates were making the most of his presence in the UK, and there had been several additions to the already crammed agenda.

Glancing at Morgen several times throughout the afternoon, Conall noticed the fine sheen of perspiration on her smooth brow when she swept back her fringe once or twice, and he thought that those arresting green eyes of hers appeared a little glassy and over-bright—as if she was running a fever. But they were already halfway through their discussion and there was nothing he could do about her condition right then—she was furiously taking down notes, and at that point the subject in hand was the lucrative Docklands project that Derek had been in charge of. Besides Derek, and lately Conall himself, no one else knew the project better than Morgen. Bringing in one of the other PAs to take over probably wouldn't be a very good idea from that point of view alone.

However, Conall proceeded to keep a close eye on his newly acquired assistant. When the break came for coffee, and people were milling around the refreshments that had been arranged in the adjoining room, leaving him and Morgen alone, he went over to talk to her.

'How are you feeling?'

He leant across her, saturating her senses with his seductively masculine scent, scrambling her brain even more than her temperature was already doing. Returning her gaze quickly to the pages of shorthand she had steadily been compiling throughout the meeting, Morgen decided avoiding those searching blue eyes was far safer than meeting them head-on.

'I'm fine. Thank you for asking.'

'You look a little flushed, if I may say so.'

'It's warm in here…don't you—don't you think?'

Momentarily forgetting her vow to keep visual contact to a minimum, Morgen found her glance suddenly trapped by his, like a ray of sunlight trapped a dust mote. No matter how hard she tried she couldn't look away for several debilitating seconds.

Breaking the spell, Conall moved first.

'I'll open a window.'

He opened a couple, deliberately taking his time, praying the rush of cool fresh air would help calm down his heightened libido. Conall knew the heat of desire as much as any normal, healthy red-blooded male, but when he looked into Morgen McKenzie's bewitching green eyes, with their sweeping black lashes, desire moved up to a whole other level. If he weren't careful this yearning to have her in his bed would become an obsession.

'That's better. Thanks.' She ran a hand round the back of her collar, where her hair was tied back, and Conall couldn't help noticing the curling tendrils of ebony silk that drifted loose around her nape. He shoved his hand into his trouser pocket to stop himself from reaching out to touch—to discover for himself if it was as invitingly soft as it appeared.

'Want me to get you some sandwiches and a cup of coffee?'

'No, thanks, I'm not hungry. Water is fine.' As if to highlight her preference, Morgen poured herself a glass of water from the jug in front of her on the table and took a sip. Her hand was not quite steady, and Conall frowned at the idea that she was finding the meeting an ordeal.

'Shouldn't be too much longer now.' Glancing down at his watch, he picked up the sheet of paper with the agenda printed on it from beside Morgen's shorthand pad. 'Five more items. I'll keep them as short as I can, and when we're done here I'll take you home.'

Conall saw the word 'no' start to form on her exquisite lips and squared his massive shoulders. There was no point in being the boss if you couldn't use it to your advantage in times of need. And right now Conall needed to know that he was driving Morgen home. He wasn't being totally selfish either. Anybody could see the woman was running a temperature. She'd nearly walked out in front of a speeding car earlier; the last thing Conall wanted on his conscience was her having an accident on the way home because she was too ill to concentrate.

Shifting uncomfortably in her seat, Morgen sighed wearily. 'I told you before—I appreciate your concern but I don't need you to drive me home. Now, please, think no more of it.'

But at five-forty-five precisely Morgen found herself being guided towards the car park and helped into the passenger seat of a luxurious sedan by a solicitous but steely-eyed Conall, who wasn't taking no for an answer—at least not today, and not from her. Resignedly, she gave him directions, and spent practically the entire journey in mutinous silence.

Why was he so insistent on taking her home? He was taking his responsibilities as her boss a little too seriously, Morgen decided. Expanding parameters he had no business expanding. Even Derek—bless him—as generous as he could be, would never have thought to drive her home because she was feeling under the weather. No, if he'd deemed it necessary at all, Derek would have got someone else to do it. But not this man.

Morgen stole a furtive glance at his handsome chiselled profile as he drove, and her insides fluttered with anxiety. As soon as they pulled up outside the house she'd make sure she had her key ready, thank him, then hurry away before he had a chance to insist on seeing her to the door—because she had a horrible feeling he was going to do just that. If she'd learned one thing about Conall O'Brien so far it was that he took his work and his responsibilities deadly seriously—no half-measures. Everything was done with absolute dedication and thoroughness. He was the epitome of the old adage 'if a job's worth doing, it's worth doing well.' Not that Morgen could fault that. It was just that right now she didn't particularly want him to apply it to her.

But by the time they pulled up outside the cheerful red door, in a street where doors were predominantly painted black or, even worse, grey, Morgen was feeling too ill to care what Conall would or would not do. She certainly didn't have the strength to worry about whether he thought the street she lived in looked rundown and poor, or whether the cars that were parked outside were several registrations older than his. All she wanted right now was her bed, and if she didn't make it as far as that then the couch would have to suffice. Thank God Neesha was at her mother's tonight, sleeping over, because she would hardly be capable of caring for her child the way she was feeling.

'Thank you, I—'

'Give me your key.'

'What?'

His expression as implacable as granite, Conall turned towards her and put out his hand.

'Your door key. I'm taking you inside, Morgen. I'm going to make sure you take some fever medication, then I'm going to make sure you get into bed. It doesn't take a scientist to see that you're burning up. I might even phone your doctor and ask him to pay you a visit.'

'Now, wait a minute, I—'

But it wasn't easy to be indignant when you felt as if your head was going to become personally acquainted with the pavement at any second, Morgen realised. Nodding with a mixture of fatigue and resignation, she dug into her bag for her keys and dropped them into his opened palm.

'There's a good girl.'

'I resent that!' Pulling him back by the sleeve of his expensive suit, Morgen glared, despite the spinning sensation in her head. 'I'm not a girl—I'm a woman!'

Conall's blue eyes darkened perceptibly.

'Sweetheart, from the minute I laid eyes on you there was never any doubt in my mind about that. Now, let's get you inside before you collapse where you sit.'

CHAPTER FIVE

AFTER negotiating a bright but narrow hallway, lined as far as he could see with prints of herbs and flowers, Conall felt his senses beset by the uplifting notes of rose and vanilla—two fragrances he knew well because of his sister Teresa's penchant for scented candles.

Morgen's house was an Aladdin's cave of sensory delights, he realised as he followed her into the living room. Much like the woman herself. Proportionally the room might have been small, but what it lacked in square footage it more than made up for in comfort. It was a room that a person could seriously look forward to coming home to, Conall decided, feeling a tug of something almost unfamiliar.

He'd thought he'd long ago put to rest the urge or the need to put down roots. To have a place and a person you loved to be there for you when you returned home from work at the end of the day was not something he'd considered for a very long time. Besides…for him it would never work. He hated to admit it, but he was too much like his father for that.

'What a lovely room.'

Although the main colour scheme was pale yellow and gold, there were splashes of bold vibrant colour in evidence everywhere. Soft red velvet and silk throws were draped across two big couches, and piles of cushions in a kaleidoscope of hues and textures spilled across every available seating space. Above the Victorian fireplace, that had clearly been lovingly and painstakingly restored, there was a huge, vivid framed print of a beautiful pre-Raphaelite model with skin as pale as milk and hair a rich and luxuriant auburn decorated with a wreath of white roses. Conall studied it briefly before switching his perusal to Morgen, suddenly alarmed that she looked barely able to stand on her feet.

'Thank you.'

Although feverish, she heard the genuine appreciation in Conall's tone, and something warm crowded into the empty space in her heart. Here was a man who had a reputation as an architect *par excellence*, who she knew had designed and built houses for the rich and famous—houses that were featured in the glossiest up-market magazines—dream houses—and yet there he stood, in the middle of her humble little living room, and professed he thought it 'lovely'. Right then, she almost cried.

'Why don't you sit down, kick off your shoes and let me get you some aspirin and a glass of water? If you don't sit down soon you look like you're going to fall down.'

She was in no position to argue. Dropping down onto the couch before Conall had even finished speaking, she kicked off her sensible leather loafers, flexed her toes and shook her hair loose from its knot.

For a moment Conall just stared at the glossy raven mass that slipped around her shoulders, then he moved abruptly to the door, once again engineering some safe distance between himself and her—because his desire to reach out and touch was almost too compelling to be ignored.

'The kitchen's just down the hall—the last door at the end. You'll find some medicine in the cupboard above the fridge.'

In the small compact kitchen, with its clean pine furniture and terracotta-tiled floor, Conall easily located the medicine, filled a glass with water, then stood momentarily transfixed by the childish drawings displayed on the front of the fridge, held in place by several colourful magnets.

He was particularly drawn to the one with a bold title in bright red felt-tip: 'My Mummy.' The surprisingly well-executed picture was of a tall slim lady with long flowing black hair, cat-like green eyes and a lush red mouth. For a long moment Conall just stood, absorbing the shock—acclimatising himself to the realisation that Morgen had a child. She was a mother. It had to follow, then, that the child had a father...Morgen's boyfriend? This Neil character? Or was the child the offspring of a previous relationship? He knew he had no right to be jealous or angry, but just then none of his feelings made any sense.

Swallowing hard, Conall made his way back down the narrow hallway to the living room, the thick sea-green carpet deadening the sound of his footfall. When he found Morgen lying on the couch, her head resting on a bank of velvet cushions, her eyes closed, his chest tightened inexplicably, and he found he needed a minute to accustom himself to the idea that a relationship with her—apart from a professional one, of course—was now totally out of the question. As much as he desired her—and even the thought made his heart pump faster—he wouldn't try to break up an already established relationship, especially not one where there was a child concerned.

As if sensing his presence, Morgen opened her eyes.

'You found it. Thanks.' Struggling to sit up, she accepted the two white tablets into her palm, then swallowed them one at a time with two big gulps of water.

'You keep a very tidy house,' Conall drawled softly. 'It makes it easy to find things. Why didn't you tell me you had a child?'

The swimming sensation in her head increased. The kitchen—of course... He must have seen Neesha's drawings on the fridge. Oh, well. Focusing her tired gaze on Conall's serious but undeniably handsome face, Morgen decided she might as well be frank with him. Under the circumstances, what else could she be? Too bad if he didn't like it. She hadn't asked him to drive her home in the first place, and she certainly hadn't invited him in.

'You never asked me, so it never came up.' Her tongue came out to wet the rosy seam of her lips, and Conall absorbed the wholly innocent little action with a fortitude even he hadn't thought he was capable of. Unbuttoning his jacket, he sat down, making himself comfortable on the second couch, every cell in his body thrumming with tension—because he wanted her. Even though she was flushed with fever, even though she had a child, even though she probably had a steady relationship...none of it deflected his passionate attraction one jot.

'Her name's Neesha. She's six years old. I didn't mention it because I didn't want to give you another excuse to imagine my commitment to work was less than it should be. That first morning, when you found me asleep at my desk? I'd been up the night before, nursing my daughter's cold; that's why I was so tired. It's well known that some bosses don't like female staff having family commitments. You'd already threatened me with the sack once, and I need this job. Now you know.'

Conall's blue eyes sharpened as he absorbed what she'd just told him. 'Neesha? Presumably she's the "favourite person" you mentioned the other day?'

Sighing wearily, Morgen pushed her fingers through

her curtain of dark hair, making Conall's own fingers itch to do the same. But he knew there was a wealth of resentment in that sigh that told him she didn't exactly enjoy explaining the circumstances of her life to him. And why should she?

'Of course. Who else would I mean?'

'Where's her father? At work?'

'I wouldn't know. We're lucky if we see him three or four times a year, if that.' A mirthless laugh broke free from her lips. 'Or perhaps I should say unlucky?'

'You're separated?' Conall couldn't deny the swift stab of hope that took a speedboat ride through his bloodstream.

'Divorced...five years ago. I'm a single parent. Now you know everything about me.' Her green eyes flashed resentment again, but this time Conall felt better equipped to deal with it.

He smiled. 'Not everything. Why did you break up?'

She made a little sound of exasperation, and if she'd been standing Conall guessed she would have shown him the door. Far be it from him to take advantage, but he was glad she was too indisposed to contemplate it. Though if he were truly the gentleman his mother had raised him to be without a doubt he would have chosen a better time to pursue this particular line of questioning.

'That's private.'

Hugging her arms around her middle, Morgen wished that he would just get up and go. Why was he hanging around, plaguing her with all these questions, when all she wanted to do was curl up on the couch and go to sleep? Simon had been a first-class bastard, but she wasn't about to reveal as much to her boss. Besides, knowing how men stuck together about these things, Conall would probably think the fault had been hers, and

Morgen had had enough judgements already to make her wary of exposing herself to more.

'Having children is hardly a sacking offence, Morgen. As long as my staff realise they do have a certain level of commitment to work, and don't take advantage, then as far as I'm concerned taking time off to take care of their kids when they're ill or be there to see a school play isn't a problem. I'm not a family man myself, but I know it's short-sighted not to acknowledge that people have another life outside work. If that's something I've been guilty of in the past, then clearly it's time for a change. Where is your daughter now, by the way?'

'At my mum's. She stays over there one night in the week.'

Despite not wanting to display vulnerability of any kind to this man, Morgen couldn't help but draw her legs beneath her and let her head slip back down onto the cushions. She was so tired. If falling asleep were an Olympic sport, she'd win it hands down. Conall would just have to see himself out. If he expected to see her at work in the morning she'd need at least twelve hours to try and shake this thing. She was glad, though, she acknowledged sleepily, that he'd said what he had about family. It made him seem much more approachable, somehow—less the high-powered charismatic architect and more like an ordinary human being.

By the time Conall got back on his feet, dragged his fingers through his hair and loosened his tie-knot, it was evident that Morgen was well and truly asleep. Scanning the room, he pulled a soft plaid wool throw from a padded Victorian armchair and draped it gently across her slumbering figure. He remembered she'd protested vehemently about being called a girl earlier, but right now, looking down into her flushed, almost angelic face, she reminded Conall of a small child that needed taking care of.

Why the very idea didn't have his feet burning a hole in the rug to get out of the door, he could only wonder. He'd only really ever dated career women: strong, capable, ambitious individuals who knew what they wanted out of life and stopped at nothing to get it. If a little warmth had been lacking in their make-up sometimes, tearing up the sheets as an extra-curricular activity after work had easily made up for the deficit—if indeed that was what it was.

'We work hard and we play hard,' a male colleague—proud to be over thirty and still single—had asserted over drinks one night. But even then Conall had experienced surprising discomfort at the generally accepted ethos. Having a reputation as a bit of a playboy wasn't all it was cracked up to be, he'd found. There was something about being able to have anything you wanted—including beautiful women—that didn't always sit right. He wasn't hankering after having a family, or anything ludicrous like that, but maybe it would be kind of nice to have one special woman in his life instead of several? As long as she didn't cling and expect him to marry her.

'You go through girlfriends as often as you change your shirt,' his sister Teresa had once scolded him, and he'd asked her why he should have any remorse about the fact when they were all consenting adults who knew what they were getting into from the start. He always made it clear from the outset that it was a short-term thing, with no strings, and the women mostly agreed. One or two had clung a little, he recalled with regret, but in the main everyone was happy. Everyone got what they wanted. Didn't they?

His chest felt curiously hollow as he continued to study

the sleeping Morgen. Clearly she hadn't got what she'd wanted, if she was divorced. Once upon a time had she believed in happy ever after? Conall found it disturbed him to think that her girlhood dreams had been crushed by a man. Despite his own aversion to the married state, inexplicably it made him feel as if the whole of his sex had let her down.

Good grief! Where was this leading? Shaking his head in disbelief, he glanced at the clock on the mantelpiece. Almost simultaneously his stomach grumbled. He hadn't eaten anything since this morning—he'd given the sandwiches at the meeting the go-by in order to stay and talk to Morgen. Trouble was, he was loath to leave her and go in search of food when she might need him. The idea that she was unwell and would have to manage on her own in the night seriously bothered him. If only he'd thought to ask her for her mother's phone number before she'd fallen asleep, instead of wearing her out with his questions. At least he could have rung her and told her that Morgen was ill. Now what was he supposed to do?

In the end he made his way back into the kitchen, telling himself that surely Morgen wouldn't mind if he made himself a sandwich. He'd pay her back by taking her out to dinner. Warming to the idea, he spread two slices of wholemeal bread with some low-fat spread he found in the fridge, then added a couple of messily cut slices of cheddar cheese. Okay, so he wasn't known for his culinary expertise, but he was hungry—what could be better than staples like bread and cheese? Now, if only Morgen had a handy bottle of good red wine, Conall thought wryly, he'd be in seventh heaven...

Stirring in her sleep, she felt every bone and every muscle she possessed seem to collectively groan in agony.

Something woolly was tickling her cheek, and Morgen blinked her eyes open in the semi-dark and pushed it away, panicking suddenly because she didn't remember covering herself with a throw before she'd fallen asleep. Conall? When had he left? And, more to the point, what had her parting words been? She could only pray she hadn't said something stupid. Something she might regret.

Pushing up into a sitting position, she peeled her tongue from the roof of her mouth and grimaced at the taste. Gasping for a drink, she swung her legs to the floor, wishing she didn't feel so dizzy and hot, trying to remember what she was supposed to be doing, because she couldn't somehow get to grips with co-ordinating her brain and her limbs at the same time.

'Steady. Let me help you.'

The low rumble of Conall's voice coming at her out of the darkened room made Morgen almost faint with shock. She stared as his hand came down on her shoulder and gave it a reassuring squeeze. What was he doing here? And what was the time, for goodness' sake? He'd removed his jacket and tie, she noticed, and a silky lock of his hair flopped across his forehead as he bent down to her.

'Where do you want to go?' he asked concernedly.

Morgen licked her dry lips and wished her limbs would stop shaking. 'To the bathroom. I can—I can manage.'

'You're burning up.' Automatically his hand moved to her forehead, swept back her fringe and assessed her temperature. 'As soon as I get you back from the bathroom, I suggest you get straight into bed. You'll have to show me where your room is.'

Struggling to her feet, Morgen felt like a newborn foal, trying to get to grips with the use of its legs. When she stumbled Conall was there to steady her and hold her, and she could have cried because she was feeling so weak and really did seem to need his help.

'You shouldn't be here,' she whispered forlornly, sniffing to hold back the tears. 'Why did you stay?'

His blue eyes didn't waver. The look that met her troubled gaze almost made her heart break. 'Because you needed me.'

It was as simple as that. No other explanations needed, clearly. Not once in the time she'd lived with Simon had he even stayed awake when she was unwell, never mind nursed her through it because she needed him. And he was a doctor.

With a sigh, Morgen allowed Conall to help her to the bathroom.

Insisting she leave the door unlocked, so that she could call for his help if she needed it, he leant against the wall in the corridor, wishing that he'd insisted she'd gone home earlier. The least he could do now was make sure everything else was all right for her. He'd tuck her into bed, make sure she had plenty to drink, and give her a couple more tablets to take her temperature down before she went back to sleep again. Then he'd spend the night on one of her silk-draped couches and see how she was in the morning.

She wouldn't like it, but she was in no condition to protest, he thought grimly. Risking Morgen's temper was a risk he was willing to take if he could see to his satisfaction that she was all right.

Switching off the light in the bathroom, Morgen told herself she felt marginally better now that she'd brushed her teeth and eliminated that dead budgerigar taste in her mouth. But it still didn't stop her from swaying slightly as she endeavoured to stay upright and fix Conall's tall broad-shouldered frame with a wobbly little smile.

'All done.'

'Where's your bedroom?'

'I bet you say that to all the girls,' she joked feebly, then wished she hadn't when Conall's handsome brows drew together in what appeared to Morgen a highly disapproving little frown.

'I prefer my women to be in full control of all their faculties before things get that specific, sweetheart,' he drawled, making all the hairs on the back of Morgen's neck stand to attention. What was the matter with her? she thought miserably. Why did she have to be so ultra-aware of this man? What was it about him that made her yearn for the impossible, even when she was ill?

'I wasn't trying to make—make a pass at you or anything.' Turning away, she almost jumped out of her skin when Conall's hand snapped meaningfully round her wrist. Staring up at him, her skin flushed with fever and her legs quaking, she was totally powerless to tear her gaze away from those intense blue eyes as they bored into hers.

'Do you think I would have turned you down if you had? Even in your present unhappy condition, I want you like I have no right to want you. Now, let's get away from the subject before I forget I'm the gentleman I like to think I am.'

In her bedroom, Conall drew the pale lemon voile curtains closed against the night and took a deep steadying breath. He'd left her sitting on the edge of the old-fashioned brass bed, struggling to remove her jacket, while he tried not to stare and imagine her undressing for him.

Already he was in a fever of his own. Being in her

room was unbelievably more erotic than any fantasy he could have conjured up himself, and he could give the average Hollywood director a run for his money in that department. The room was ultra-feminine and made Conall acutely sensitive to his own opposing masculinity. The women he usually dated mostly seemed to prefer a fairly minimalist look in the bedroom, but Morgen's room was a seductive assault on the senses. As well as being filled with the most erotic scents—sandalwood, and something sweetly exotic he couldn't identify—everything around him was a feast for the eyes.

In one corner of the room was a dressing table draped in white muslin, covered with lots of pretty Victorian scent bottles and a silver hairbrush and comb set. The floor was covered in a pale gold-coloured carpet, with an Oriental oval rug by the bed, and in the centre of the ceiling hung an old-fashioned brass chandelier with tear-shaped droplets made of crystal. But it was the bed that drew Conall's attention, and the thought of her in it would haunt his dreams. Covered in virginal white linen, it was an inviting contrast to the midnight darkness of Morgen's hair, and he couldn't help the heat that inflamed him when he imagined making love to her in that bed, that dark silken mass spread out on the pillow behind her.

'Can I get into bed now?'

She'd peeled back the white covers and was starting to crawl beneath them when Conall moved across to stand beside the bed, his casual stance belying the tumult of desire raging inside him.

'You've still got your clothes on,' he reminded her, stern-faced. 'Where are your night things?' He stared, half expecting her to produce a long lacy Victorian nightgown from beneath her pillow.

'I feel too ill to get changed,' she protested. More to the point, she had no intention of putting on her nightclothes with Hunk of the Year standing there watching her.

'You'll regret it in the morning.' Now there was a faint suggestion of a smile ghosting his lips, and Morgen felt her insides teeter as if she was riding a unicycle on a high wire.

'Well, then, you'd better leave me to it.'

As she started to swing her legs onto the floor again, Conall gave her a gentle shove backwards. Ignoring her indignant glare, he let his hands drop to his hips. Morgen's gaze did too, and she gulped when she realised what she was doing.

'Where are your things? I'll get them for you.'

Jerking her head towards the heavy Victorian chest of drawers on the other side of the room, Morgen reluctantly told him, 'Third drawer down. You can't miss them.'

She was right, Conall mused, handling the red silk pyjamas in awe. They were so soft they felt like water trickling through his fingers. Desire slammed hard into his groin, and for a few moments he stood perfectly still to ground himself. She wore red silk pyjamas in bed. What was she trying to do? Torture him?

'Put them on,' he instructed, throwing them onto her lap, his voice gruff. 'I'll wait outside.'

CHAPTER SIX

MORGEN was lying in bed staring up at the ceiling when the door swung open and, unannounced, Conall strode in. He was bearing a glass of water on a tray and his hair looked tousled and damp, as if he'd just showered. Around his jaw was the distinct dark shadow of a beard. With his shirt undone to almost the centre of his chest, and minus his tie and jacket, he looked almost too disturbingly attractive for words. Like a living, breathing male calendar cover.

For a moment Morgen couldn't speak, she was so tongue-tied, and if it was possible her temperature soared even higher. Apparently he'd stayed the night—just as he told her he would. She still couldn't quite believe it.

'How are you feeling this morning?'

She didn't mince her words. 'Like death warmed up, if you must know.'

'Here, take two more of these.' Carefully positioning the tray on the small muslin-covered nightstand beside the bed, Conall proffered the tablets, then handed her the glass of water to wash them down with. He waited patiently while she took them, then put the glass back down onto the tray.

'You're still very hot.' Sliding his hand onto her brow, he frowned at the evidence. 'There's no way you can come into work today. Perhaps I should call the doctor out? Have him check you over?'

Morgen wasn't used to this much attention when she was ill, and she still couldn't quite believe that her high-powered boss had stayed the night in her humble little house to watch over her and make sure she didn't get any worse. Protecting his firm's investment, maybe? Or were his reasons even more basic than that? His statement that he wanted her more than he had a right to had played over and over in her head during the night, as if she'd left her finger on the 'rewind' button of a tape recorder. But he could want all he liked, she thought defiantly. It didn't mean that he could have. She had her child's welfare to consider before she went racing down that old road of heartbreak again, and that was where she'd be headed if she became intimately involved with her boss.

There was also the little matter of her ex-husband's behaviour in the past—surely that was enough on its own to prevent her from getting any silly ideas about a relationship with Conall? High-powered men were too into their careers to really dedicate themselves to a proper relationship with a woman—let alone a woman with a child. And hadn't she heard Conall say with her own ears that he would never let a woman get really close? Top of Morgen's list of priorities was raising her daughter, and she wasn't about to indulge in some hot little affair, possibly jeopardising her job and her relationship with Neesha. Even if the idea was getting harder and harder to resist.

'I don't want you to call the doctor. There's nothing he'll suggest other than what I'm doing already anyway. I'll wait until lunchtime and see how I feel, and if I've improved, I'll jump in the car and drive into work.'

'Over my dead body!' Conall's searing blue gaze was like a laser beam boring into Morgen's skull. 'Thank heaven your car's still at work—remember? But even if it was possible, I'd tie you to the bed first to stop you doing it! Be sensible, Morgen. Stay put for the rest of the day and make sure you don't venture any further than this room and the bathroom. Unfortunately I have several meetings scheduled for this afternoon, and I need to do some background work to prepare, otherwise I'd stay with you. Have you got a phone nearby?' he asked.

Morgen reached across to the nightstand at the other side of the bed for the slim white cordless phone that she always kept there.

'Right here.'

'Keep it handy. I'm going to be ringing you on and off throughout the day, just to make sure you're okay. I might also have to ask you where I can put my hand on things I need at the office. That all right with you?'

'Of course.'

Their business concluded, Morgen was worryingly bereft of words. It didn't help matters when Conall stood staring at her as if he was having great difficulty in walking away. A little muscle ticked in the side of his jaw. It seemed to trigger a series of worryingly sensual tremors in her body that she was helpless to do anything about. Imagination was a powerful thing, Morgen silently warned herself. Conall O'Brien could have any woman he wanted, most probably. Why on earth would he be interested in a single mother and all the baggage that automatically entailed? And now he'd seen her at her worst—oh, no! She hadn't even glanced in a mirror this morning—never mind brushed her teeth or combed her hair—she must look like Dracula's mother!

'Thanks for bringing me home, by the way, and for staying the night. I hope you weren't too uncomfortable on the couch.'

'I was fine. I used your shower—I hope you don't mind? I need to go home now, for a quick shave and to get a change of clothes. I've made up a flask of soup for you in the kitchen—I went through the cupboards and found some tomato and lentil. Make sure you have some if you feel hungry. And ring me if you need anything. That clear?'

He made her feel like a little girl again—that much was clear. Safe and protected—*cherished*, almost—a seductive combination for any woman overdue for a little tender loving care. Morgen smiled her gratitude, even though her head felt as if all the rock drummers in the world were having a jamming session inside it.

'Are you always this thoughtful for your employees?'

Ignoring her question as though it made him uncomfortable, Conall strode back to the door. 'And ring your mother—just to let her know you're not well. I'll see you later.'

And with that he was gone. Morgen dropped her head back against the pillows and gratefully shut her eyes.

His senior associate's PA was pleasant and helpful to a degree, but she wasn't Morgen. And she couldn't make coffee he wanted to drink. Scowling for the umpteenth time that afternoon, Conall glanced up at the slender blonde bearing down on him with yet another cup of the undrinkable brew and forced a smile.

'Thanks, Julie. By the way, did you find that file I asked you for?'

'I'm still looking for it, Mr O'Brien. Could you bear with me for a few more minutes?'

'I need that file if I'm to address this item at the meeting in half an hour. Do your best to find it, will you?'

When she'd closed the door behind her Conall sighed and tunnelled his fingers through his already besieged hair. He needed a haircut, but when he was supposed to fit it into his already impossible schedule he didn't know. Finding himself reaching towards the telephone, he snatched his hand away at the last moment.

He'd already rung Morgen three times. The last time she'd sounded sleepy and husky-voiced, and he'd suffered uncharacteristic guilt because he knew he'd just woken her. If she was going to get back to the office sooner rather than later, he really should let her rest. Trouble was, she'd pricked his conscience with her unstinting concern over Derek, and her accusations to the effect that Conall lacked compassion when it came to his staff's personal problems. Morgen had probably resigned herself to the fact he was a cold, uncaring, arrogant swine.

He winced at the thought. She was a single mum coping on her own. That had to be hard. Even though his own high-octane lifestyle was probably a million miles away from hers, he knew that. But, aside from her provoking his conscience, he missed her. Crazy when he'd only known the woman for just a few short days, but there was no explaining this powerful attraction he seemed to have developed for her.

Every time Conall closed his eyes, even briefly, he saw her in those sexy red silk pyjamas. Last night, when he'd checked on her at around one in the morning and found she'd kicked off the covers and her pyjama top had rolled revealingly up to just beneath her breasts, Conall had sucked in his breath at the sight of her gorgeous sexy midriff.

His friend Mike back at the New York office would no doubt advise him to take her to bed as soon as possible and nip this wild attraction in the bud before it got out of control. Perhaps that was what he should do? Morgen might not exactly like or admire him, but he knew she wasn't entirely immune to him either. It wouldn't be too hard to seduce her, surely? Not a man of his experience…

'Concentrate, O'Brien! What the hell is the matter with you?' Furious with himself, he pulled the drawings spread out on the desk towards him and forced himself to run through them one more time. The door opened as he did so and Julie's blonde head appeared.

'Did you want something, Mr O'Brien? I thought I heard you talking.'

What I want right now, I can't have… Conall's blue eyes stared unseeingly ahead, then he gave himself another mental shake and flashed a broad smile at his temporary PA that had her clenching everything in her body that could possibly be clenched.

'I'm fine. Just thinking out loud,' he said apologetically, then got to his feet to go and stare out of the window as she closed the door behind her again.

'I didn't see your car parked outside.' Lorna McKenzie fussed around her daughter's bedside, rearranging the glass of water on the tray, patting down the soft embroidered counterpane.

With a daughter's radar, Morgen picked up the slight note of suspicion lacing her voice. 'A friend from the office drove me home. My car's still in the car park at work.'

'You should have rung me. I would have come and got you myself. Did this "friend" of yours think to ring the doctor for you?'

It was typical of her mother to assume that nobody else knew how to do anything properly. Briefly shutting her eyes, Morgen silently warned herself not to rise to the bait. When she opened them again her mother was staring down at her, lips slightly compressed and arms folded.

'I didn't want the doctor to come out. It's probably just a viral thing. It'll blow over in a couple of days.'

'And what if you need some proper medication? I suppose you're going to treat yourself with some of those alternative remedies of yours instead?' Lorna sighed and unfolded her arms. 'You are the most stubborn creature on the planet, you really are! Have you managed to eat anything?'

'My friend made me up a flask of soup.' She'd had some earlier, but hadn't felt much like eating.

She wondered what Lorna would say if she knew this 'friend' she kept referring to was actually her boss. The head of the firm, no less. To tell the truth, Morgen was still having trouble getting to grips with the fact that Conall seemed so genuinely concerned about her well-being. Already he'd rung her three times today, and, worse than that, she'd found herself actually looking forward to those calls. Just hearing his voice had given her a resurgence of energy that was better than any medicine—orthodox or otherwise. Dangerous...

'Well, I'm going to make you a nice chicken stew. Neesha's already had tea, but she can have some stew as well later, if she's hungry.'

'What's she doing now?'

'Watching a video. I've told her you need to rest. She's already done her homework, and it's all packed away in her bag for tomorrow. I'll send her in to see you in a while. In the meantime, why don't you try and get some more sleep?'

Morgen made a face, wishing her head didn't feel as if it had a lead weight wedged inside it. 'I don't want to sleep any more. I think I'll just put on my dressing gown and go and sit with Neesha.'

'Well, don't blame me if you start to feel worse later. You just won't be told, will you?'

'For God's sake, Mum! I'm twenty-nine years old, not five! If you stopped treating me like a child and just let me make my own decisions things would be a whole lot happier all round.'

Planting her feet on the floor, Morgen reached for her silk wrapper, pulled it on and headed for the door. Lorna stared after her, her eyebrows arched and her expression wounded, as it usually was when her daughter chose not to take her advice.

'That would be fine if you made a few *right* decisions now and again,' she muttered.

Morgen knew the wise thing to do would be to ignore such a remark. But hurt and anger welled up inside her like a dam about to burst and completely sabotaged such wisdom. Her green eyes furious, she dropped her hands to her hips as she glared at the older woman.

'And what's that supposed to mean? We're not talking about Simon again, are we, by any chance? He left me, remember? He's the one who didn't want the responsibility of fatherhood—so don't act like it was all my fault. Do you think I wanted to be a single mother? You know how hard it's been for Neesha and me, yet you still bang on about bloody Simon like he's the injured party in all this!'

'You could have hung on to him if you'd really wanted to.' Patting down her soft brown hair, Lorna met her daughter's furious look with an aggrieved one of her own.

'Hung onto him?' In disbelief, Morgen's mouth dropped open. 'What exactly is that supposed to mean?'

'You're an attractive woman. It can't be beyond you to work that one out for yourself. You've forgotten how to be feminine since you've been working; that's your trouble. You think you've got to be the tough career woman, act like a man to get what you want, when the reverse is true. Simon was besotted with you. If you'd only used that to your advantage, instead of letting his parents push him around, he'd still be here with you now.'

Swaying slightly, Morgen stuck out her hand and held onto the doorjamb. Because she was so angry her head started to swim even more than usual. And deep down inside she felt betrayed. Betrayed because her mother seriously seemed to believe that she had somehow driven her husband away because she'd refused to use her feminine wiles to keep him interested. Lorna just wouldn't see the truth. Simon's parents had never believed her good enough for their beloved son, and eventually he'd believed that to be the case too—even when she'd become pregnant with his child.

'We weren't good enough for the likes of Simon Vaughan-Smith and his ˙family, Mum. You, me, Neesha...that's the cold, hard truth! We weren't good enough! Why can't you just accept that and move on? What did you expect me to do? Act like I was grateful he'd even noticed me, because he was a doctor and I a mere secretary? Was I supposed to bury my self-respect for the sake of a wedding ring?'

'You're every bit as good as him and you know it!' Sniffing, Lorna pushed past Morgen into the hallway. She turned slowly, digging for the little square of linen tucked into her sweater sleeve. 'I just want you and Neesha not to have to struggle. What harm can it do for a mother to want a good man to look after her daughter?'

Morgen's green eyes glittered as she looked at Lorna, heartsore. 'Simon wasn't a good man, Mum,' she said softly. 'He was a weak man. Neesha and I are better off without him. Things aren't so bad. I earn a reasonable salary, we live in a nice house, I manage to keep our overheads to a minimum most of the time and I've even managed to accumulate some savings. All in all, we don't do badly.'

'No, you don't,' Lorna agreed, dabbing beneath her eyes. 'But you work long hours and don't get to see enough of your child. Who's the one who's been to see her last three school plays? Me. Don't you think Neesha would prefer it to be you, Morgen?'

Already feeling guilty about that, and other similar situations when her mother had had to stand in for her because she was working, Morgen sighed heavily. 'Well, perhaps I can do something about that, at least.' She was remembering what Conall had said about realising that people had a life outside work—about it not being unreasonable to expect to be there for your child's school play.

The charismatic head of O'Brien and Stoughton Associates was a good man—Morgen instinctively sensed that to be true, even if his manner was a little on the brusque side. Perhaps while he was in the UK she could talk to him about cutting down some of her hours here and there, so that she could be more flexible where Neesha's needs were concerned? She'd certainly put in her fair share of overtime since Derek had had his problems. Surely the firm could pay her back by cutting her a little slack?

As soon as she was feeling better she resolved to ask Conall for a meeting. Protocol probably dictated that she go via Human Resources, but why do that when she had a God-given opportunity to talk to the head man direct?

'I'll talk to them at work,' she told her mother now. 'I'll see if I can change my hours round a bit, swap over to flexitime or something. Don't worry, I'll sort something out, I promise.'

'You know it's not because I don't want to look after Neesha, don't you? I love that little girl as much as any grandmother could love her grandchild. I just think that you and her deserve more time together as a family. She's growing up so fast, Morgen. I don't want you to miss all those special times, because they'll never come again. All I want is for you both to be happy.'

Sliding her arm around her mother's thin shoulders, Morgen pressed her close with tears in her eyes. 'I know that, Mum. I know that.'

'Morning!'

Immersed in deep conversation with Richard Akers, one of the senior associates, Conall did a double-take when Morgen's dark head appeared briefly round the door.

'Excuse me, Richard. I'll be back with you in a moment.'

Emerging into the outer office, he stared in amazement at Morgen's busy slender figure as she bustled around her desk, picking up mail, sifting through it, dropping some of it into her in tray and holding onto the rest. She was wearing a red fitted jacket over a white silk top and a knee-length black skirt, her lovely long hair tied back in a sleek ponytail with a slim red ribbon. Had she lost a little weight? Conall's blue eyes narrowed in concern, even though he was secretly fiercely glad to see her.

'And what, may I ask, are you doing back in the office

today? I thought we'd agreed you weren't coming back until after the weekend?'

'I was feeling fine this morning, so I thought I might as well come in. Shall I put some coffee on?'

'Forget the coffee,' Conall growled, acutely conscious of the fact that Richard Akers was waiting in his office, and that the man wasn't known for his patience, yet anxious to reassure himself that Morgen was well enough to be back at work. 'Stand still for a minute, will you?' Pushing his fingers through his hair, he glared at her.

He'd had a haircut, Morgen observed. That edge she'd noticed about him when she'd first met him was definitely back in evidence. As well as looking every inch the successful architect he was, from the top of his expensively cut hair to the tips of his stylish Italian loafers, the air around him seemed to bristle with the power he emanated—as if she were standing on a ley line. Her heart gave a nervous little jump.

'What's wrong?'

Her lower lip had trembled slightly and Conall honed in on it like radar. His whole body seemed to suddenly snap into super alertness. Why was it that work was the furthest thing from his mind when she was around? He'd seriously have to address that little problem if they were going to continue to work together in any sort of harmony.

'Nothing's wrong. I just want to establish that you're actually well enough to be here. What did the doctor say?'

'I didn't go to the doctor. I'm quite capable of judging for myself whether I'm feeling better or not. We give the medical profession far too much credence, in my opinion.'

'Well, you still look a little peaky to me.'

'I'll be fine when I get back into the swing of things.' Her gaze slid guiltily away.

To tell the truth she was still feeling a little under par, but that was surely to be expected after three days in bed and only two after that of being up and about. And she had no appetite to speak of, which was probably why she was looking a little peaky, as Conall had put it. But still, he didn't need to know that. Besides, Neesha was at school during the day, and Morgen had been going a little stir crazy cooped up in the house all by herself. Lorna had dropped by intermittently, of course, but Morgen had persuaded her that she was on the mend and really didn't need fussing over. Work seemed more appealing than it had for a long time. Nothing to do with the fact that Conall O'Brien was there, of course...

'We'll talk when my meeting with Richard Akers is finished.' Striding back to the door of Derek's office, Conall paused to give Morgen a final once-over. Satisfied she would last the day without doing herself some long-term damage, he smiled briefly. 'Don't overdo things, and, yes, I'd like some coffee when you've got a minute.'

'I'll see to it.'

Finding her chair before her legs gave way beneath her, Morgen put her hands to her burning cheeks and sighed. How was it possible for a totally innocent little smile from that man to reduce her to a quivering, shivering wreck? Even Simon, handsome as he undoubtedly was, had never been able to provoke such a violent response in her.

Being glad to be back at work because she needed to get out of the house and back into a routine was one thing—but being glad to be back because of a certain six-foot-two, broad-shouldered, gorgeous blue-eyed male who happened to be her boss was completely another. If she was going to survive the remainder of the time he was acting as stand-in for Derek Morgen was going to have to claw back some professional distance between them.

She was seriously going to have to forget the fact that Conall had rung her every day since she'd been ill at home—and not just to discuss work either. Those phone calls had done her self-esteem a power of good. Not that she'd ever dream of telling him that. All such a confession would accomplish would be to turn their relationship into something more personal than she could handle, and Morgen could not risk such an eventuality. Socially and professionally she and Conall were light years apart—just like she and Simon had been. Never again would she put herself in a position of not feeling good enough. When—and if—she ever contemplated a relationship in the future, she'd be looking for someone who was her equal on every level. Someone she could totally be herself with.

Picking up the morning's post, she tore open the first letter with her small silver knife with unnecessary zeal, then endeavoured to concentrate hard on reading the contents.

CHAPTER SEVEN

MUCH to Conall's growing frustration, he hardly found an opportunity to have a conversation with Morgen all day. There were meetings scheduled in his diary practically back to back, and on top of that he'd spent the afternoon at the Docklands site with Stephen Ritchie and the contract manager, dealing with a particularly sticky problem that had come up. By the time he arrived back at the office it was five forty-five, and Morgen was reaching for her raincoat.

She looked startled when he blew in through the door, and her cheeks went very pink. Conall grinned. He threw down his briefcase onto the nearest chair.

'Still here, Miss McKenzie?' he teased. 'If I didn't know better I'd think you were trying to impress the boss.'

'Seeing as I'm here most days until at least six or six-thirty, that would be an incorrect assumption on your part, *Mr* O'Brien.' Colouring again, Morgen hastily slid her arms into the sleeves of her navy blue raincoat. 'If you're intending on staying a bit I've left the percolator on simmer in your office. Don't forget to switch it off before you go. Well…have a good weekend. I'll see you on Monday.'

'Hey! Not so fast.' Snagging her wrist as she breezed past him, Conall shut the door behind them and manoeuvred her deftly against it.

She felt as if her heart was about to jump straight out of her chest, and her green eyes flew wide in alarm. He was too close—didn't he know that? Breaking all the rules of office protocol, as if he didn't give a damn. If someone should walk in right now he'd be— But how could they walk in when her back was against the door?

Her mind raced wildly as she tried not to notice those enviably long lashes of his, the beautiful sweeping cheekbones and the bristly shadow of a beard starting to form around his hard jaw. As for his mouth—well, there was no good reason on earth why she should fantasise wanting to kiss it, was there? Just because his lips looked firm and commanding and seemed to promise a sensuality that only a woman who'd lost the will to live wouldn't crave…that was a poor excuse for feeling her resolve crumble, wasn't it?

'What—what is it?'

'I want to see you tonight. Have dinner with me.'

'I can't.' Panic locked Morgen's throat. It was impossible…not to mention dicing with death. She was already experiencing the kind of urges and longings that could get her into big trouble, and if she wanted to make her life any more complicated then she was going about it in the right way.

'Why not?' Quirking a dark eyebrow, Conall loomed closer. Morgen gulped.

'Because—because I always spend Friday night with my daughter. We order in pizza and watch *Top of the Pops* together.'

'Sounds nice. What about tomorrow night?'

'I told you when we first met that I don't get involved with people from work. It's the one rule I don't break.' Tipping up her chin, Morgen challenged him to find something wrong with her reasoning. Surely even he could see the sense in her explanation? One day he might even thank her for it.

'Never been tempted? Even once?' Gravel-voiced, Conall ran his finger down the length of her nose, then drew the pad of his thumb gently round her plump lower lip, as if he were examining something quite exquisite and unique.

Heat assailed Morgen as if she was lying on a beach somewhere with the sun beating down. A slow trickle of perspiration slid inexorably down her back. 'Tempted' was the word. Knowing the soft gasp she heard had emanated from her own lips, she struggled to maintain control, to act sensibly. *Move away*, a small voice of caution in her head advised, and Morgen obediently slid her hand around Conall's wrist to push him away.

That was her first mistake. His flesh was warm and firm beneath her touch, and the fine dark hairs on the back of his hand felt like silk. The contact immobilised her. In desperation she raised her soft green eyes to his.

'I don't—I don't want to be tempted to do something I might regret. I don't want to lose my job when things get complicated—and, believe me, they will. Nothing good ever comes out of office romances, and I have a living to earn and a child to think of.'

'Do you always play safe?' Conall's brow puckered as if the idea really bothered him. 'It doesn't leave a lot of room for spontaneity, does it? Let down a few barriers, Morgen. I won't tell…I promise.'

His mouth was on hers before she could think another thought. Melting warmth throbbed through her body and her whole world suddenly existed only in those marvellously warm and pliant lips of his, expertly coaxing hers into a response that she was helpless to withhold any longer. His kiss was deeply stirring, and filled her with the most sensual longing she could imagine. Hot little tingles of delicious pleasure sizzled up and down her spine.

Welcoming his deeper exploration, Morgen's tongue danced with his, discovering erotic little sensations of velvet and fire with a hint of rich roast coffee, and her heartbeat throbbed like distant drums in her ears as her body found a natural home against the solid male hardness of his.

Breaking the kiss to press his lips against the side of her throat, Conall wound his fingers through her hair, tugging at the silky red ribbon that held her ponytail in place. He groaned when he freed the heavy dark velvet strands and anchored his hand possessively behind her head.

'I think wanting you has become an obsession with me,' he confessed huskily.

His words sent terror of a very particular kind barrelling into Morgen's heart. Simon had always been so disappointed with her sexual responses. Many times he'd accused her of lacking passion. Saying that as well as being his professional inferior, she was also useless in bed—another strike against her suitability as a wife. The memory robbed her of all her pleasure. Especially now, in this too intimate situation with Conall. Already they had gone too far, transgressed boundaries between the professional and personal that they shouldn't have crossed. Was it too late to put the brakes on? Morgen wondered in panic. Could she extricate herself from this wildly impossible attraction to her boss without causing either of them further embarrassment or difficulty?

'I'm sorry, Conall.' Breathing hard, she pushed him away, momentarily thankful for the fact that her hair had tumbled loose around her face because now she could partially hide behind it. 'You're a very attractive man, but I'm not interested in sex with you. I don't doubt that you could have any woman you set your sights on…you're rich and successful with no ties, and I'm a divorced single mother trying to make ends meet. I can't afford to throw away everything I've worked for in the heat of the moment. I have a child, Conall. I need to work to support us both. I need this job. Do you think I'd be so foolish as to jeopardise it for a one-night stand with my boss?'

'Why would you think for a second that your job would be under threat if you slept with me?'

'Because inevitably it would be. It would complicate things. How could it not? We'd see each other every day and it would be—it would be too distracting, for one thing. It would make it impossible for me to work here. I'm not the kind of woman who takes sex lightly, Conall. If you think I am then you've made another wrong assumption about me.'

'And what makes you think that all it would be between us is a one-night stand?' Frustrated and annoyed, Conall stepped back and yanked at his tie-knot.

Leaning against the door for support, Morgen stared. 'What are you saying? That you're looking for a relationship?'

He couldn't answer her truthfully right then, because he didn't know himself. He'd hardly thought beyond taking her to bed and fulfilling the fantasy that had gripped him since he'd first set eyes on her. Consumed by dreams of her that nightly took over his sleep, he wanted a release from such sweet torture. He knew his track record with women wasn't good, and that he had no experience of a long-term relationship. But right up till now it hadn't seriously bothered him. Not when 'short and sweet' had always been his motto. So *did* he want a relationship with this woman? Was he prepared to break one of his own major rules and commit to her long-term? She had a child to take care of. If he wanted Morgen, he would have to start considering her daughter too…

'No.' Answering for him, and smiling to hide her hurt, Morgen straightened and then bent to retrieve the slender red ribbon that lay curled on the floor at her feet. When she stood up again her pretty green eyes had a glaze in them that hadn't been there before. 'I didn't think so. Well, that's fine with me, because I'm not looking for a relationship either. I've already messed up royally once in my life; I'm not in a hurry to do it again. Goodnight, Conall. Enjoy your weekend. I will.'

He let her walk away, silently cursing himself because his wits had apparently deserted him. Why had he taken so long to answer her perfectly reasonable question? He wasn't some insensitive oaf. He should have known from the beginning that she wasn't the type of woman who was into brief sexual flings, even if he had jumped to the totally wrong conclusion when he'd first seen her. He'd quickly learned that she was conscientious and loyal and very clearly put her child first. That much was evident. Just the kind of candidate his mother would label 'marriage material.' He groaned. He didn't want to marry anyone. To Conall, 'long-term' meant more than four or five dates—not a lifetime commitment.

Not wanting to examine his feelings any further right now, he reached for the telephone on Morgen's perfectly tidy desk. As he dialled, he picked up a notepad that was lying there and idly flicked through it. On the first page he opened, he read: 'Saturday, buy Neesha new shoes, then take her to Tumble Drum 2 till 4.' Frowning, Conall tried to decipher what the last part meant as the ring tone purred in his ear.

'Hello?'

'Mother? It's Conall. Are you home tonight?'

'Conall! At last! I was wondering when you were going to get in touch. Of course I'm home. My bridge evening was last night. I'm just in the kitchen, preparing myself a meal. Why don't you come and join me?'

Knowing he'd put off seeing her for long enough, and partly glad of the opportunity to just kick back and relax with someone who knew all his little foibles as well as he knew them himself, Conall dropped the notepad he'd been handling to tap his fingers resignedly on the desktop.

'Okay. I'll see you in about an hour. I'll bring a bottle of wine.'

'Conall?'

'Yes, Mother?'

'Are you all right, dear? Your voice sounds a little strained.'

Sexual frustration, no doubt. Smiling ruefully, Conall sighed into the phone. 'I'm fine. Busy day, that's all.'

'Well, come over and put your feet up. It will be wonderful to have your company.'

As he let the receiver settle firmly back onto its rest Conall realised with surprise that he echoed the sentiment.

'So, you're enjoying being back home?' Victoria Kendall's crystal-blue eyes, so reminiscent of her son's, carefully considered the big man filling the armchair opposite her own.

Hearing the hope in her voice, Conall grimaced. He knew only too well where this conversation was probably leading. But he'd enjoyed a wonderful home-cooked dinner, and two generous glasses of good Chablis, and he was feeling predisposed to be kind. At least that was what he told himself as he replied.

'Yeah, I'm enjoying being back home. There are some things that I've missed for sure.'

'Then why don't you think about buying yourself a place in town? I know Teresa doesn't mind you staying at her flat, but it's not really practical if you're going to be working at the London office for any length of time, is it?'

'The thought had crossed my mind.'

In fact, on the drive over to his mother's Conall had thought of not much else…well, apart from Morgen, that was. But somehow buying a house and his feelings for the woman were inexplicably intertwined. Worrying.

'Seriously?' His mother beamed at him. 'So you really might think about working from the London office permanently?'

'I didn't say that.' Vaguely disgruntled, Conall got to his feet and paced the floor. 'There's a lot of things to consider before I make such a decision.' *Like, how soon can I tell them in New York that I'm transferring back to the UK?*

He wondered how Morgen would feel about that. When Derek returned to the fold she'd no longer be working directly for Conall, but what was to stop him promoting her? After all, he'd need an assistant of his own if he were to work at the London office permanently, wouldn't he? The idea shouldn't hold such ridiculous appeal but, God help him, it did. After that sexy knee-trembling kiss they'd shared earlier he was in no hurry to put an ocean between them any time soon. Even if she did think his motives were less than worthy.

'What's on your mind, son?'

Gently, Victoria came up behind him, the softly stirring classic scent she always wore drifting around him, bringing an unexpected memory of his childhood.

'I know something's bothering you. Call it a mother's intuition.'

'Nothing's bothering me. Least, nothing that a good night's sleep won't cure.'

Victoria put out her hand and touched his arm. 'It's a woman, isn't it?'

A mother's intuition? Next she'd be telling him she had a crystal ball.

'You're like a terrier with a bone, you know that?' But even though he scowled humour flashed in Conall's compelling blue eyes. Delighted, his mother didn't bother to hide her pleasure at the thought her son had finally met someone he was prepared to get serious about.

'Who is she? Where does she live? She must be a local girl if you're thinking of moving back here.'

'Don't jump to any conclusions. I'm not the settling-down type, as you well know.'

'Like father, like son, huh?' Victoria rolled her eyes and shook her head, but not before Conall saw the brief flash of hurt reflected there.

He admired and loved both his parents, but it was true that when it came to relationships he'd taken his lead from his father. Desmond O'Brien hadn't been able to resist playing the field even when he'd married. Eventually, worn down by her husband's philandering ways, Victoria had filed for divorce, but not without deep regret, Conall knew. In her heart she still carried a torch for the man—even now, when he was living on some tropical island thousands of miles away with a woman thirty-five years his junior.

'We're not going to fight, are we?' Guilty and irritated, Conall turned away.

Frustrated, Victoria 'hmmphed' and crossed her arms in front of her soft pink cashmere sweater. 'I know you don't like me drawing comparisons with your father, but just look at the way you conduct your relationships, will you? And I know you've avoided coming to visit me because you hate hearing me say it. I would have given that man everything, Conall...everything. And I did for a while. But he chose to throw it all back in my face with his tawdry little affairs with other women. Don't you want someone special in your life? Someone who'll commit to you and you only? How long do you intend playing the field just because you can? Where is the satisfaction in that? You're thirty-six years old now. About time you started thinking of marrying and having a family. I'm sixty next birthday and I don't want to be too old to enjoy my grandchildren.'

What would his mother think if Conall told her the woman he was crazy about already had a six-year-old daughter of her own? The thought came out of nowhere, and a surge of anger made him push it away again. He didn't want a permanent arrangement with Morgen. All he'd wanted from the very beginning was to get her into bed. That hadn't changed—no matter how different or sweet she was compared to the other women he'd known. She was a single mother and Conall knew nothing about children. Brief as his relationships were, he liked his women to think of him exclusively. He was far too selfish and egotistical to want to share her with her daughter.

'Let's change the subject, shall we?' Affecting a yawn, he dropped back down into the armchair he had recently vacated. 'Let's talk about *your* love-life for a change, Mother. A little bird told me that a certain good-looking widower who's joined your bridge club has been showing more than a passing interest in you lately.'

Blushing like a girl, Victoria fanned her suddenly warm cheeks. 'I'll give that sister of yours a piece of my mind when I see her next! "Good-looking widower" indeed!'

The place was hot, noisy and colourful, and Neesha's excitement at being taken to the Tumble Drum all but poured out of her as she stood jigging around next to her mother. Once they'd paid, and Neesha's name had been logged in the visitors' book, Morgen wound her way past plastic tables and chairs to the front, near where the climbing frames and soft play areas were situated. Then she pulled up a chair, sat down and began helping Neesha take off her shoes.

Two little girls, both in jeans and T-shirts, raced by holding hands and Morgen saw her daughter's pretty face light up. 'There's Chloe and Lily. They're both in my class! Can I go and play now, Mum? Can I?'

She was off like a rocket through the wooden swing gate before Morgen had a chance to steal a kiss and warn her to be careful. She had a mother's natural tendency to spot danger everywhere, but tried not to be too uptight about it and transfer her anxieties to Neesha. Finally, satisfied that Neesha had found her friends and was off climbing a rope ladder in the jungle area, Morgen left her things on the table and went to buy herself a much anticipated cup of tea from the cafeteria.

She'd enjoy having a few minutes to herself while Neesha played with her friends, and if her thoughts happened to stray back to yesterday and that kiss that Conall had floored her with, then it was only natural and who could blame her? Even if he'd made it perfectly clear that he only wanted to get her into bed and nothing more.

*   *   *

He was completely out of his depth. As he stood scanning the colourful chaos all around him Conall knew if his rich corporate friends could see him now they would swear he had taken leave of his senses. And without a doubt they would be right. To pursue a woman on a visit with her daughter to a children's indoor play arena just because he had the hots for her was not something he would normally ever have contemplated. But Conall had had to throw out his rule book where Morgen McKenzie was concerned, and now, God help him, he was definitely in uncharted territory. He'd even lied to the girl at the check-in desk just now to gain access, telling her that he was Morgen McKenzie's boyfriend, come to meet her and Neesha.

'Whoa! Steady!' His long legs almost buckled as a sturdy young boy suddenly careened into him out of no-where.

'Sorry, mister!' With an apologetic grin the boy was off, chasing after his friend before Conall had got his bearings back.

'They didn't warn me I'd be taking my life into my hands coming in here,' he muttered to himself as his gaze settled on the huge play area full of ropes and ladders, swings and slides.

Where were Morgen and her daughter? Calling at her house on the off-chance, he'd sent up a silent prayer of thanks when he'd found her mother in residence. Once Lorna McKenzie had established Conall was who he said he was, she'd helpfully given him directions to the Tumble Drum and had been only too eager to assure him that Morgen would be there at least until four o'clock.

Spying some empty tables near the front, he made his way towards them, wondering how parents coped with all the noise and the chaos but inwardly experiencing unexpected pleasure at the sight of so many delighted children clearly enjoying themselves. As he was about to sit down on one of the white plastic chairs Conall did a double take.

On a bouncy castle, amid several small girls and boys, was Morgen. Dressed in faded blue denims, belted round her shapely hips with a fringed suede belt, and a tight pink T-shirt that exposed her midriff, she was bouncing up and down with the children as if she was one of them, long dark hair flying and her cheeks flushed with heat. He also couldn't fail to notice that her exceptional breasts were bouncing nicely along with her. Heat slammed urgently into his groin and Conall felt his heart stall in his chest. Was there a sexier or more beautiful woman alive?

Feeling the chair behind his knees, he sank down slowly into it, content to just sit there and watch. What she'd say when she saw him he didn't know, but right now he didn't care. It was enough to just sit and admire the object of his desire at his leisure, and when he heard an appreciative comment from a father sitting behind him with another male friend Conall smiled to himself, knowing he wasn't the only one who was enjoying the impromptu floor show.

Still out of breath from her recent exertions, Morgen froze when she saw the big confident male lounging in one of the white plastic chairs just by the swing gate. In his classic-cut denim jeans, blue chambray shirt, boots and tan suede jacket, he stuck out in the sea of parents and children like a sore thumb—surely he'd be more at home in some trendy up-market wine bar than in a converted industrial unit that had been transformed into a children's play park? What on earth was he doing here? And how had he known where to find her?

Finally able to get her limbs to move once more, Morgen took her time reaching his table, her lips pursed and her green eyes flashing clear disapproval.

'Well, well, well. All this time and I never guessed you were a parent.'

'All this time and I never guessed you like to get so…' Conall's provocative gaze slid deliberately up and down her figure and back again to her face '…physical.'

Heat bloomed in Morgen's already flushed cheeks and throbbed right through her body down to her toes.

'What do you think you're doing here? And how did you know where to find me?' She sat down opposite him in a huff, and Conall had to force himself to peel his gaze away from the luscious shape of her breasts outlined by the tight-fitting T-shirt.

'I wanted to see you this weekend. I dropped by your house and spoke to your mother; she told me where to find you. We need to talk. Specifically, about what happened yesterday.'

'Yes, well, the whole point is that it should never have happened in the first place.' She stuck out her chin, daring him to argue with her. What was wrong with him, for goodness' sake? Couldn't he see that their association was fraught with pitfalls? He owned the firm she worked for! He moved in entirely different circles from her. He'd seen where she lived, so he could be under no illusion as to her personal circumstances. What was his game? Why was he pursuing her like this?

'I'm afraid I can't agree with you.' His deep frown drew his smooth brows together, and Morgen found herself wishing those unsettling blue eyes of his weren't quite so blue…then maybe she would have a chance of staying immune from his charm. Yeah, and the government would declare that everyone should work a three-day week with full pay...

'I'd really like us to see each other outside of work,' he told her.

'And when did you decide this? Yesterday you didn't seem very sure.' Folding her arms across the plastic table, Morgen leant forward a little as she asked the question. For a long moment Conall was simply bewitched by the beauty of her face.

'You know I'm very attracted to you. And if that little kiss we shared was anything to go by I'd stake a bet that you feel the same way about me. So let's knock down a few barriers, Morgen, and come clean. I want you. I want to spend some time with you, and not just in bed. I'd like to get to know you and your daughter better. Are you willing to give me that chance?'

CHAPTER EIGHT

'I DON'T take chances where my child is concerned. I can't afford to get involved with you, Conall, however fleetingly. My first priority is as a mother. I've tried the relationship thing and, apart from having Neesha, came off the worse for trying it.'

Feeling a sudden chill descend on her, Morgen leant back in her chair. Trying to sound as if she meant what she was saying was difficult when the man sitting opposite her was consuming her with his long slow gaze, making her stomach do cartwheels and stirring up feelings she wasn't sure she wanted stirred up.

'So what are you saying? You're never going to have a relationship with a man again?' Despite feeling frustrated with her reasoning, Conall couldn't help a rueful grin. 'That's like showing a kid the biggest box of chocolates in the shop and then telling him he can't have one.'

'For once in my life I'm putting me and Neesha first. Children need stability. Our lifestyle may not be ideal, but it works for us, and that's the way I like it.'

'So what happened between you and Neesha's father? I take it he's the one who made you so anti-men?'

Morgen was discomfited by the fact he made her sound as if she had a personal vendetta against his gender. 'I'm not anti-men. I just don't particularly want one in my life right now. I need all my energy just to do what I have to do. And I'd rather not talk about Simon, if you don't mind.'

To be perfectly truthful, Conall didn't particularly want

to talk about Morgen's ex-husband either. Whoever he was, and whatever he'd done, he'd made a big mistake letting Morgen go, as far as Conall was concerned. Colossal. Conall wasn't the marrying kind, but if he had made such a commitment to Morgen he was damn sure he would have done everything in his power to honour it—despite his mother's insistence on comparing him to his father.

His whole body went on alert every time he was near Morgen—his senses so consumed by her presence that all he could think about was his need to make her his. For the past week, every morning his first thoughts had been of her, and then at night there'd been the dreams... If this went on much longer without resolution he'd be investing a serious amount of cash in therapy.

'Well, let me buy you a cup of coffee at least.'

He started to get up from the table, but Morgen slid her hand across his to stop him. As soon as she touched him she cursed herself for being so stupid. The man was sexual dynamite and her heartbeat was off and running like a greyhound out of its trap. Their gazes met and locked, and helplessly Morgen's fingers curled around Conall's. The connection was so profound it shook her.

'Mummy, I need a drink!'

Guiltily she snatched her hand away as Neesha drew up breathlessly beside the table. Her dark hair clung to her forehead in tendrils and she looked excited and happy. Morgen felt a strong wave of love and pride suffuse her.

'So this must be the lovely Neesha?' Smiling broadly, Conall studied the beautiful child with interest. No need to wonder which parent she got her looks from. Neesha shyly dipped her gaze, then moved closer to her mother.

'Darling, this is Mr O'Brien—the man I'm working

for at the moment. He wanted to speak to me about something so he came to find us.'

'You can call me Conall,' he told her, his expression somewhere between a frown and a smile, ridiculously disappointed that Morgen had introduced him to her child so formally. 'And isn't this a great place? They never had anything like this when I was growing up.'

'Didn't they?' Her natural curiosity vying with her shyness, Neesha stared interestedly at the man she'd seen holding her mother's hand.

'We had parks and museums and stuff like that, of course, but this must be great—especially when it's raining outside.'

'I can climb right to the top of that platform and swing on that rope.'

Conall's gaze followed the direction of her finger, his blue eyes widening in pretended amazement.

'Wow! That's a pretty big achievement for a little girl like you.' He grinned. 'Seems like us boys have some stiff competition in the playground these days.'

'Isn't that the truth?' Morgen's lips curved in a knowing little smile and her eyes glinted with amusement.

If he'd been standing next to a volcano about to erupt Conall couldn't have got any hotter. He had to remind himself exactly where he was, because his first instinct at the sight of that heavenly smile was to haul her into his arms and kiss her until his lips went numb. Not a good idea, under the circumstances, he mused ruefully. Not with Morgen's pretty little daughter studying him intently, as if she was trying to fathom him out.

'Let me buy you a drink. What will it be?' Glad to have a distraction other than Neesha's beautiful mother, Conall reached into his jeans pocket for his wallet and got to his feet.

'You don't have to do that.'

'I want to. Do you mind?'

Morgen gave a little shake of her head. 'No. She'll have some blackcurrant juice, please, and I wouldn't mind a cola. It's thirsty work getting in touch with your inner child, believe me.'

'If you promise to get in touch with your inner child one more time on that bouncy castle, just for me, I'll buy you as much cola as you can drink!' Chuckling out loud at the mortified look on Morgen's face, Conall made his way to the cafeteria.

Thinking of the friends he usually hung around with socially, he reflected that this visit to the Tumble Drum with Morgen and her daughter possibly beat anything he'd done with them hands down. In fact, he couldn't remember the last time he'd enjoyed himself more.

'Can I help you with that?'

Startled, Morgen glanced up from the plate she'd been rinsing and wondered what little devil of mischief had prompted her to invite her boss to dinner. Perhaps it was because she'd been so sure he would refuse? She'd been certain he had far better things to do on a Saturday night than spend it with her and Neesha, but yet again he had surprised her.

Turning up unexpectedly like that at the Tumble Drum was one thing, but agreeing to share pasta and meatballs in front of the TV, watching Neesha's video, was something she hadn't really been prepared for. Now, as Morgen watched his perfectly relaxed figure monopolising her narrow doorway, she wondered how long he would stay before telling her he had to go. It alarmed her intensely to realise she was in no hurry for him to leave.

'I'm just rinsing them to stack in the dishwasher,' she

explained, tucking her hair behind her ear and blushing slightly.

'It was a great meal. Thank you.'

A sexy dimple at the corner of his mouth, Conall smiled, and Morgen immediately wished he wouldn't. It was a weapon that never failed to miss its target, she was sure, and could probably entice her into things that could get her into all sorts of trouble. She was certain she wasn't the first female to fall for it either. How many women had been so expertly seduced by that gorgeous smile? Victoria Kendall, for instance…? And how had that lady felt when Conall hadn't shown up that night for dinner and sent her yellow roses instead? Morgen knew how she personally would feel. Crushed.

'You must be easy to please,' she quipped self-consciously. 'It was nothing special. But pasta and meatballs are Neesha's favourite, I'm afraid.'

'Then your daughter has good taste. The movie was great too. I don't think I've enjoyed myself so much in a long time.'

'Really?' Drying her hands on a clean teatowel, Morgen leant back against the sink to face him. Every nerve in her body seemed to quiver at the very sight of him.

'Why look so surprised?'

'They're such simple pleasures.' Shrugging, she threw the teatowel down onto the drainer. 'A man like you must—'

'A man like me?'

To her alarm, Conall moved across the kitchen towards her. His glance was very direct and extremely potent. Beneath it, Morgen felt as if her spine had just melted like hot candle wax.

'Just what kind of man do you think I am, Morgen?'

'Not the kind of man who eats pasta and meatballs in the front of the TV with a six-year-old girl and her mother—not usually, anyway. You're probably much more used to five-star hotels and restaurants. You're the head of a premier firm of architects and it's obvious you move in very different circles to me.' Heat surged into her face and her eyelashes fluttered self-consciously downwards.

'And that bothers you?' Conall asked speculatively.

'You start out thinking those differences don't matter...' Her throat tightening, Morgen wished the ghosts of the past would leave her alone. Simon was history. She should have got over how he'd made her feel a long time ago. She shouldn't let feelings of inadequacy ruin her future...or her present. But that was easier said than done. 'But they do.' Her voice cracked. 'They do.'

'Not to me, they don't.' All of a sudden his big muscular body was very close—just a hair's breadth from her own, in fact. Morgen felt her breath hitch as those sensual blue eyes of his gazed hungrily down into her upturned face. 'You're a beautiful, intelligent woman, Morgen. Any man would be proud to know you. No matter where he came from or what he did. Don't you know that?'

Her lip trembled and she sank her teeth into it to quell it. Seeing the gesture, Conall tilted her chin towards him, then dropped a gently experimental kiss on her mouth. Morgen's eyelids automatically closed to absorb the full intensity of his touch. That featherlight kiss reverberated throughout her body like a small but deadly explosion, and set up such a longing inside that she trembled with the force of it. When she opened her eyes again Conall was studying her as if he was really seeing her for the first time. Almost as though her soul had been laid bare to him.

'Whatever it is you've got, Morgen McKenzie, you could bottle it and make a fortune.'

She placed her palm on his chest. Her hand looked very pale and slender, outlined by the sky-blue chambray of his shirt, but it was his heat that undid her. The warmth of his body seemed to burn right through the material.

'Do you say that to all your girlfriends?'

'I can honestly say I've never said that to another woman in my life. And I'm not seeing anyone else at the moment, if that's what you're asking.'

Morgen hesitated before asking the question that had been on her mind throughout the evening.

'What about Victoria Kendall? The woman you got me to send flowers to the other day?'

'What?' A wide smile breaking free, Conall looked heartbreakingly handsome as mirth lit up his eyes. 'Victoria Kendall is my mother.'

'Really?'

'She reverted back to her maiden name after she got divorced from my father.'

'Oh.' Relief flooded Morgen's insides. She wanted this man, but she wouldn't succumb to this tempestuous attraction if he were seeing somebody else. There were certain standards she very definitely wouldn't transgress.

'Happy now?'

'Happiness is such a fleeting thing. It doesn't last.'

'Then live for the moment. Hmm?' His arms sliding seductively round her waist, Conall wished fervently that he could banish every trace of sadness from her beautiful green eyes. He couldn't ever remember feeling that way about any other woman, and he'd dated many.

'So, Miss McKenzie…where do we go from here?'

It was difficult to think straight with the sudden rush of blood to her head. Her expression revealing her anxiety more candidly than she knew, Morgen glanced nervously up at Conall. 'Where do you want to go from here?'

Overwhelming her with another sexy smile, he tightened the strong arms around her waist a little. 'Want me to be frank with you?'

Morgen nodded.

'Your bed would be good.'

She dipped her gaze, her heartbeat going crazy. She knew she should do the sensible thing and say no, but she was suddenly tired of her enforced self-restraint. After six years of celibacy, her body ached for a man's attentions. And not just any man. Only *this* man would do…this dark-haired, blue-eyed giant who had 'heartbreak' written all over him. Right then, Morgen thought her heart was worth the risk.

'All right, then.'

He watched her tug her tight pink T-shirt over her head in the lamplight. Impatience overpowering him, he took it from her and threw it on the bed. The white lace cups of her uplift bra presented her beautiful curves like a sensual banquet, causing heat to flood Conall's body at the sight, making him immediately heavy and aroused. When Morgen reached for the snap on her jeans, his hand waylaid her and jerked her towards him.

His kiss was almost ruthless—all worthy intentions of taking things slowly helplessly abandoned in the heat of passion. Weaving his fingers through her long dark hair to anchor her more firmly to his embrace, Conall let his hand shape and mould her heavenly curves, thoughts of possessing that beautiful body making him a little crazy. He'd staked his claim and—barring acts of God—had no intention of letting her go any time soon. Feeling her tremble, Conall exulted in his manhood, his only desire to pleasure them both in a way that neither would forget in a hurry. He had been aching for her from the moment he'd set eyes on her, and if he'd nurtured any fantasies at all about his perfect woman, Morgen was the living, breathing manifestation of that fantasy.

Sliding his hands down her slim back, he deftly released the catch on her bra, sending up a silent prayer of thanks that he'd accomplished it without difficulty, then removed it completely. It too joined the discarded pink T-shirt on the bed. Her breasts were as lovely as he had known they would be. Voluptuous and womanly, with dusky nipples that just begged for his mouth to pleasure them. Making a little sound of need, Morgen wound her arms around Conall's neck, pressing those same luscious breasts deep against his chest.

'Let me finish undressing you,' he whispered huskily against her neck, and she willingly let him do as he desired, her skin quivering wherever he touched her. When she was naked, he laid her back on the bed and stripped off his own clothing.

Morgen reached out in wonder to caress the flat brown nipples on his magnificent chest, her fingers diverting to push through the springy dark hairs surrounding them. His body was amazing. Wide smooth shoulders, with enough rippling musculature to die for, that incredible chest tapering down to a hard flat stomach, lean hips and long, well muscled legs—now tangling with hers. She sucked in her breath, letting his kiss devour her, the hands that explored his powerful male body as eager to stroke and touch as his own were in pleasuring her.

Conall's movements were instinctive, yet skilled, and he seemed to know exactly where to touch her to elicit the utmost pleasure. He also knew the exact pressure to apply to make her gasp, and Morgen arched her back off the bed, truly believing she would lose her mind if he didn't possess her right now.

Above her in the lamplight, Conall stilled. His blue eyes seemed to burn into her heart with the intensity of his stare. 'I hate to be the voice of reason, but I really need to protect you.'

'Have you—? I mean, did you—?' It was a bit late in the day to be struck dumb with embarrassment, but Morgen was. How could she have been so mindless as not to think of it herself? Was she so eager to bring trouble crashing down on her head?

But Conall was reaching down to the end of the bed for his jeans, withdrawing the requisite protection from his pocket and sheathing himself adeptly. Morgen's heart slowed to beat at a more normal rate. Thank God. Thank God he'd had the foresight to be sensible before things had gone too far.

Moving above her, his big body covered hers, and she slid her long slender arms around his neck then, with a hungry sigh, eagerly received his kiss. As his mouth moved tormentingly over hers, taunting and teasing, nipping and caressing, Conall let one hand slip down her body to part her legs. Morgen had been ready for him practically from the moment he'd suggested they go to bed and, seeing no reason to postpone their mutual pleasure, Conall eased his way inside her, his satin length filling her until Morgen thought she might lose her mind with the intense gratification of it.

'Wrap your legs around me,' he ordered, and she needed no second bidding.

He drove into her hard, his hips grinding into hers as his mouth took possession of first one nipple then the other, nipping and suckling so that Morgen felt the deep primeval connection convulse like lightning from her breast to her womb. Then she was digging her fingernails into that strong muscular back, the tips of her fingers sliding on skin slippery with perspiration, holding on for dear life as he took her over the edge to an intensity of bliss she'd never experienced before. With a fierce groan that seemed to take him by surprise, he quickly joined her. The weight of his body drove her deep into the bed, but there was pleasure in that too, in being held captive in those big strong arms, feeling those slick hard muscles contract beneath her fingers.

Emboldened by his loving, Morgen pushed back his dark silky hair as he raised his head to look down at her, her heart almost stalling in her chest when he smiled.

'You are definitely the nicest thing that's happened to me in a long time, Miss McKenzie.'

'You're not so bad yourself, *Mr* O'Brien.'

'Just one question.'

'What's that?' Morgen gasped as his mouth temporarily captured one of her fingers and sucked on it.

'Why wasn't I informed that the woman of my dreams was working right under my nose, so to speak?'

'Hardly under your nose when you work in New York,' she reminded him, a smile raising one corner of her softly curving mouth.

'My mistake. My *big* mistake.' His voice husky with delight, Conall stole another deeply hungry kiss. When he raised his head again his expression was more serious. 'As soon as I can finalise things with the New York office I'm transferring back to London permanently. Did I tell you?'

Morgen stared. 'No. You didn't tell me. Can you do that?' Her brain racing with all the implications of Conall working permanently in London, she absent-mindedly traced a circle on his bicep.

'Sweetheart, I can do anything I damn well please, seeing as I own the firm.'

Something in Morgen's mind snapped to immediate attention. What was she thinking of—being so delighted that Conall was transferring back to London? They'd just made love, and it was wonderful, blissful, the best thing that had happened to her in ages, but she couldn't allow herself to get swept along with what was happening between herself and this man. He'd just delivered a very timely reminder of who he was, and she was under no illusion that they would enjoy more together than a brief passionate affair.

Men like Conall O'Brien did not commit to women like her—she only had to think of Simon to understand that—and Conall was not a man who had long meaningful relationships with women; that much she did know. Okay, so she'd heard it on the office grapevine, and usually she held no truck with gossip, but this was different, wasn't it? How could she ignore his past track record under the circumstances? This was her livelihood she was possibly playing with—hers and Neesha's. She couldn't afford to lose her job because she'd had sex with her boss. When Conall tired of Morgen—and she was certain he would—and moved on to the next attractive woman, where would she be then? She'd die if she had to see him every day at work, knowing she'd just been a temporary distraction to while the time away now and again.

'Why did you become an architect?' she asked him, hungry for anything—any snippet of information that she could use to point out the insurmountable differences between them—to tell him why a relationship between them just wouldn't work. Because, God help her, he'd stirred up a wild impossible longing inside her that just wouldn't be tamped down, despite her profound reservations on the wisdom of it.

'My father was an architect.' Kissing her fingers one by one, he smiled down into her eyes and made Morgen's heart melt. 'Even as a child I was fascinated by what he did. And when he used to drive me past the buildings he'd designed, and explain to me how he'd go about working on ideas, I was hooked. When he retired I'd already been working for him for about ten years, so I was happy to take over the reins. His partner James Stoughton had retired a year earlier, so I was really the logical choice.'

'And it didn't faze you? The responsibility of taking over your father's firm?'

Seeming amused by her question, Conall grinned. 'No. I knew I could do it. Why should it faze me?'

'You've obviously never been hampered by a lack of confidence. When did you become so sure?' Her hungry gaze roved his face, examining one impossibly handsome feature after another, finding no flaws. Even the tiny lines fanning out from beside his eyes and the deeper grooves bracketing his mouth were fascinatingly compelling to Morgen.

'I've never really thought about it.' Frowning at her, Conall cupped her face between his hands. 'Why so many questions, hmm?'

'We've just made love.' Lifting her shoulders, Morgen tried to ignore the sudden longing that was sweeping relentlessly through her body all over again. 'I hardly know anything about you. That doesn't seem right, somehow.'

'What does seem right is you and me together like this. When I've made love to you again you can ask me all the questions you want…deal?'

As his mouth hovered bare inches from hers, his passionate words intoxicating her and for the moment driving out her fears, Morgen was powerless to do anything else but agree. 'Deal,' she whispered as his lips descended.

CHAPTER NINE

FEELING like a schoolgirl creeping out of the dorm at midnight for a snack, when everyone else was fast asleep, Morgen pushed open the door of the airy modern office, almost dizzy with relief when she saw that she was clearly one of the first to arrive. All was quiet, save for the distant hum of recently switched-on computers down the hall, and in her personal domain—the domain she was sharing with Conall—everything was just as they'd left it on Friday night.

Quickly hanging up her coat, then unpacking her sandwiches and shoving them into a desk drawer, she planted herself on her chair and with her hands pressed up against her temples gave herself a few moments to recoup.

She'd slept with her boss, and it had been a magical never-to-be-forgotten experience, but today she had to work with the man and try to pretend it had never happened. Because when she'd woken on Sunday morning the space in the bed beside her had been ominously empty. No note, no 'see you later' kiss—nothing. He'd left without so much as a by your leave. Taken what he'd wanted and gone. For the sake of her own self-respect, she now had to keep a particularly cool head. Not let him see that his desertion in the early hours of the morning had left her hurt and confused, even though she'd guessed that that was probably the way it was going to be.

It was too late now for recriminations; that much was clear. The deed was done and she had to accept the consequences. At twenty-nine years old, a divorced woman with a six-year-old child, Morgen was no wide-eyed innocent. She knew how things worked in the world of office relationships. Basically, you got involved with a colleague at your peril—because sooner or later your personal relationship would start to infringe on your work. One of you would end up leaving if things turned sour— or working life could turn into a nightmare.

Neither was a scenario that Morgen particularly wanted to contemplate, so she would assure Conall that she wasn't about to make any claims on him or make him feel awkward in any way, and no doubt he would breathe a grateful sigh of relief. All that talk about transferring permanently to London had clearly been just that—talk. Most men would say what they thought a woman wanted to hear after they'd made love.

Morgen sighed into her hands. If only he had been a man of honour, as she'd hoped he'd be. Walking out on her on Sunday morning had been pretty low. He didn't deserve to get off scot-free just because sleeping with her clearly meant nothing to him.

Still, it was pointless getting herself all worked up about it. She couldn't see how it would serve her at all. No: if she got even the smallest opportunity today, she'd force herself to tell Conall that it was okay. He wouldn't have to walk on eggshells around her, or feel he'd taken advantage. She was a grown-up and she would act like one. Whatever the fall-out from Saturday night, Morgen told herself she'd handle it. Even if her heart ached because she'd believed him when he'd said that he wanted to see her again, that he was transferring back to the London office—that she was the nicest thing that had happened to him in a long time.

Voices in the corridor made her sit up smartly and reach for the pile of work in her in-tray, but her glance gravitated automatically to the door as Conall swept into the office, closely followed by his colleague Richard Akers.

'Good morning, Miss McKenzie.'

The formality of his tone hardly surprised her, but it still hurt. Silently acknowledging it was probably for the best, Morgen felt her emotions thrown into further turmoil when she saw him wink conspiratorially, one corner of his mouth kicking up in the suggestion of a smile. Her heart did a cartwheel.

'Morning.' Addressing her response to both men, she wasn't surprised that Richard Akers barely glanced at her. Instead he preceded Conall into his office, his dour face unsmiling. The man had a reputation for being of a bit of a sourpuss, but for once Morgen didn't let it worry her. She was too busy walking on air because Conall had winked at her. Pathetic.

The meeting with Richard dragged on for two interminable hours, during which time Conall had to hand it to the man for surely being the champ at making mountains out of molehills. No wonder Derek Holden had been driven to drink if Richard had been his main point of contact day to day!

He'd started off the day feeling eager and optimistic, but now he felt distinctly ratty and in dire need of at least two large mugs of Morgen's excellent black coffee. Not to mention an even greater need to see the woman herself. That was if she was even speaking to him.

He could have kicked himself for leaving early on Sunday morning, without waking her up to say goodbye. If he'd wanted to give her the impression he was some kind of heartless lothario, playing fast and loose with her feelings, then no doubt he had succeeded. His actions had been almost automatic, he was ashamed to admit, but he'd also felt an absurd sense of panic that his life was suddenly taking a direction he wasn't sure he was ready for. He'd needed to walk and think, and then walk some more. Exercise always helped to get his head together, he found.

He'd spent the whole day trying to straighten out his thoughts. By the time evening had rolled around he'd pretty much made up his mind that he was going to give a relationship with Morgen a proper chance. Having reached that momentous decision, Conall had discovered an urgent need to ring her and let her know that Saturday night had surpassed all his expectations about making love with her. Unfortunately, Morgen hadn't been in when he rang, and even though he'd persisted late into the evening to try and contact her, her phone had just rung on, unanswered. It had irked him that she didn't even have an answer-machine to pick up a message, and he'd resolved to speak to her about that just as soon as he had the chance.

Consequently he'd spent the rest of Sunday wondering where she was all this time—and who with? He knew he was falling for her hard, but right now he had no intention whatsoever of pulling back. Instead he was absolutely resolved to see how things might pan out, for once in his life willing to let a relationship with a woman run its course without anticipating a break-up. *My, my… how the mighty are fallen.*

The sight that met his eyes when Conall stepped into the outer office had his mouth splitting in a grin from ear to ear. Morgen's very cute, very shapely rear end, hugged by her slim black skirt, was wriggling beneath her desk as she apparently searched for something.

'Need any help?'

The sound of Conall's deeply amused rich tones had Morgen bumping her head on the underside of her desk in shock. Feeling her face flame red, she moved out of harm's way and quickly rose to her feet.

Her dark hair was yet again escaping from the confines of its loose knot, drifting across her heated face in feathery wisps of silk. The desire that had seized Conall's body at the sight of her delightful derrière beneath the desk became almost painful.

'I was looking for my fountain pen.' Raising the slim gold pen aloft for him to view, before placing it back on the desk, Morgen struggled to conceal her embarrassment. Of all the undignified moments for him to walk in and find her... 'It was a present from Neesha and I didn't want to lose it.'

'I can understand that.' Moving in closer, Conall reached out to touch her hair.

Jerking back in surprise, Morgen wiped her palms down her skirt, then nervously tucked her blue silk blouse more securely into her waistband to cover her confusion.

'I was just about to come in and make you some coffee. I didn't get a chance earlier, when Richard Akers was with you.'

'Well thank God he's gone now.' Conall winced. 'That man could bore for England.'

Morgen tried to smile, but somehow her facial muscles wouldn't work. He overwhelmed her, that was the trouble—scattered her thoughts with just a glance. But she could hardly afford to have her wits scattered when he'd clearly demonstrated by leaving early on Sunday morning that she had just been a diversion for him...nothing more. Long years without knowing a man's touch had left her vulnerable to the first man she'd really been attracted to since Simon, and now she had to pay the price. If only he wouldn't stand there looking at her, with that sexy little smile of his playing havoc with her senses and driving her heart wild.

'Don't I warrant even the smallest kiss hello?' Unabashed, Conall closed the gap between them to slide his hands up her arms. Trembling with nerves, Morgen stole an anxious glance at the door.

'No. You don't. I got the message loud and clear on Sunday, when I woke up and found you gone, that what we had was just sex…a one-night stand. But don't worry, Conall, I'm not going to make things difficult for you. Some of us know how to act with a little dignity.'

'I know how it looked.' Flushing beneath his tan, he ruefully shook his head. 'But I had a lot of thinking to do about you and me.'

'And what brilliant conclusion did you come to?' She couldn't help it if her voice was scathing. His actions had made her feel cheap…*used* and cheap. Even if the sex had been great.

'I decided I want a chance at a proper relationship with you. That includes getting to know Neesha. I tried to ring you Sunday night and explain but you were out.'

'I had a headache. I unplugged the phone.' There was no thaw in the chilly tone of her voice.

Conall's steady blue gaze didn't waver. 'So? What do you think about what I just said?'

'What do I think?' Morgen pulled away from him, crossing her arms angrily across her chest. 'I think you're spinning me some kind of line, Conall. Do you know how cruel that is? You can sneer all you like at people like Derek, who care too much, but at least I don't think he'd ever consciously use anyone.'

'I didn't use you!'

'No?' She tilted her head to one side and her glance

was bitter. 'Then what do you call having sex with a woman and leaving her the next morning without so much as saying goodbye?'

At the realisation that things weren't going entirely the way he'd planned, Conall raked his fingers frustratedly through his hair. 'I've never had to pursue a woman in my life,' he admitted, gravel-voiced. 'The fact that I've done all the chasing now must surely tell you that it means something more than just sex? What other man would pursue you to a children's play park, for God's sake? I'm serious about us, Morgen. I want us to have a proper relationship. Why won't you believe me?'

'Because I don't trust you.' There. She'd said it. Funny how it didn't make her feel any better.

To give Conall his due, he did look crushed. So he was a good actor…a past master, no doubt, at manipulating women to get his own way. It wouldn't be hard, a man who looked as good as he did.

Suddenly Morgen felt very tired of all these games.

'I've got work to do.' She glanced edgily towards the door again, anxious to bring this awkwardness between them to an end, her heart thumping at the idea that their relationship was a 'no-go' after all. Something told her she wasn't going to get over the crushing disappointment that easily.

'So you're not going to give me a chance to put things right?'

'There's nothing to put right. We're both adults. I knew what I was doing as much as you. Forget about it. I know I will.'

'Liar.'

She found herself suddenly hauled hard up against his chest, and Morgen's senses were all at once consumed by him. Her mouth parted in a little inrush of breath as she saw the blue irises turn almost black, and felt his hands tighten commandingly on her waist. Where he'd all but crushed her against him her nipples ached, and tightened unbearably, already anticipating his caress, helplessly remembering his mouth on them, the heat, the longing, the way he'd made her feel…

'Do really think you can forget about me so easily?'

Lowering his head, Conall dropped a combustible little kiss at the juncture between her neck and her collarbone. The sizzling fall-out burned her all the way down to her toes and back again, and Morgen had to clamp her teeth down hard on her lip to stifle her groan.

'You're a ruthless man, Conall. Right up until now I never knew how ruthless.' Wrenching herself free from his embrace, she bumped into the desk and, flustered, picked up some papers on the pretext of studying them.

'Because I go after what I want?' he demanded, scowling.

Morgen felt the little prickle of perspiration on her brow and sucked in a deep breath. 'Because you don't care who you hurt in the process,' she said softly.

She was wrong, Conall thought bitterly. He was more than aware of the fact that he had hurt her with his apparently casual behaviour on Sunday, and desperately wanted to make amends. If he could turn back the clock and undo his leaving he would do it like a shot. He didn't want to lose this woman. He knew it would be his own fault if he did.

Blue eyes narrowing in concern, he straightened the cuffs on his shirt and blew out a breath. 'I don't want to hurt you, Morgen. If I acted like a jerk on Sunday it was because up until now I've not been entirely easy with the idea of commitment. But I don't want to let this chance with you slip away. What do you say we give things another go? Take it one day at a time, huh?'

He knew by her expression she was wrestling with the idea. Holding onto his breath, he was on tenterhooks as he waited for her answer.

'You weren't just using me?'

His heart thudded almost to a stop. 'I swear.'

'Don't think that I'm unaware of your reputation.'

His dark brows came together at that. 'Oh? And what reputation would that be?'

Uneasy at this new turn in the conversation, Morgen glanced nervously towards the door again. 'Look, Conall, I know you don't go in for long-standing relationships, and I'm not blaming you. I never expected… I mean, don't think that I'm going to make things awkward or difficult for you. What happened, happened. Perhaps it's for the best if we just put it behind us and be adult about this.'

His blue eyes turned wintry. 'I thought you didn't pay attention to gossip? You've obviously heard things that make you doubt my intentions, and you don't believe I can possibly be serious about us.'

'Right now it's hard to know what to believe.'

Again, Conall found he was cursing himself for walking out on her. Now he had his work cut out convincing her he wasn't the amoral bastard she obviously thought him to be.

'You're right. We need to talk properly. Now's not the time or place, but we need to do it soon. Can you get your mother to sit with Neesha tonight?'

Her smooth brow puckering, Morgen thought quickly. 'Probably. Yes…yes, I'm sure she wouldn't mind. But why?'

'I'm going to take you out to dinner so we can talk

like civilised adults, away from the office and away from the gossips. I'll pick you up about seven-thirty. That okay with you?'

Morgen nodded, her head in a whirl. 'Fine.'

'Good. In the meantime I'd be grateful if you could make some coffee…oh, and if you could get those notes transcribed from the board meeting last week and let me have a look at them, that would be good too.'

The door shut behind him with an ominous 'thunk', leaving Morgen staring down at the papers in her hand, wondering why she couldn't make head or tail of a single word.

At seven forty-five that evening, dressed in her one and only 'little black dress,' her make-up applied as perfectly as she could manage it, Morgen sat on her couch sipping anxiously at the small glass of dry white wine she'd poured herself. Okay, so he was late…it didn't mean he wasn't coming, did it?

The last thing he'd said to her before she'd left for the night was that he was going to drop in at the Docklands site for a brief meeting with the contractor before making his way home. He'd booked a table at some fancy restaurant in Chelsea for eight o'clock and had made her promise to be ready on time.

'Well, I'm ready, Mr O'Brien,' she said out loud into the silence. 'Where are you?'

When eight o'clock came and went, with still no sign of Conall, Morgen went resignedly into the kitchen and threw the remains of her half-drunk glass of wine into the sink. There was an awful ache in her heart, and her thoughts were tumbling over one another to be heard. Why hadn't he kept their date? Had he had second thoughts after what she had said this morning? Had he too come to the conclusion that a relationship between them was not such a great idea after all?

The pain of rejection hit her like a fist in her stomach. Hunching over the sink, she stared unseeingly into the enamel basin, fighting to keep the sting of tears at bay, vowing to stay strong even though her heart was breaking. All she could do was thank God things hadn't got too serious—at least Neesha hadn't grown to care for Conall and he wasn't yet a part of her life, as he might have been had things between him and Morgen progressed. *More's the pity…*

Finally, resigning herself to the inevitable, she wiped her eyes with the back of her hand, switched off the light, then got her jacket and car keys and drove to her mother's to fetch her daughter.

Arriving early the next morning, she was relieved to find no sign of Conall. Telling herself she was grateful for the breathing space, Morgen tried to distract her racing thoughts with work. She switched on her computer, logged on to the programme she used for minutes of meetings, then endeavoured to concentrate on the notes she'd transcribed yesterday but hadn't had the chance to type out.

Yesterday had turned into one of those days when things got steadily busier as the day wore on, and she hadn't been able to get the promised notes to Conall as he'd requested. Thinking about that, she fell into anxious speculation about the man himself. Where was he, and why hadn't he turned up for their date last night? He hadn't even had the decency to ring her and cancel. He'd let her down for the second time. She wouldn't give him another chance.

Chewing heavily down on her lip, Morgen read the

typed sentence on the monitor at least three times more without making the least bit of sense of it. Was this a foretaste of things to come? Was she destined to spend her future working days with this man feeling like some lovesick schoolgirl? Thrown into confusion when he was around, her stomach churning like crazy when he wasn't?

'Hi, Morgen.'

She glanced up as Julie hurried into the room, frowning when she saw her fellow PA looking flustered.

'What's up?'

'You haven't heard?'

'Heard what?'

'About what happened to Conall?'

Morgen's stomach lurched wildly. 'What are you talking about?'

'Last night at the Docklands site. He slipped on some scaffolding and fell. He spent the night in hospital with a cracked rib and a bad gash on his shoulder that needed twenty stitches.'

'Where is he now?' Pushing to her feet, Morgen stared anxiously at the blonde girl. Why hadn't someone informed her? But then, why should they? As far as everyone else knew she was only his temporary secretary. And to think she'd spent the whole of last night silently castigating him for not turning up for their date, when all the time he'd been lying injured in the hospital. Her stomach rolled over at the thought. She couldn't bear the idea of that strong, fit man in pain and alone in hospital.

Glancing curiously at Morgen, Julie flipped open the pad she was carrying and tore out a page. 'He's gone back home to his sister's flat in Highgate. He rang me on my mobile this morning and asked me to tell you to go over there. Here's the address. He's got some instructions for you.' She handed Morgen the torn-out page, and her blue eyes widened a little when the other woman all but snatched it out of her hand.

'Thanks, Julie. Can you take my messages? I'll phone you just as soon as I'm on my way back.'

Grabbing her coat and bag, Morgen hurried to the door.

'Give him our love.' Grinning sheepishly, Julie came up beside Morgen. 'Tell him all the girls in the office are wishing him better.'

'Sure.'

Not sure at all that she would tell him any such thing, Morgen hurried down the corridor to the lift.

He opened the door to her dressed in jeans and a light blue shirt opened halfway down, exposing the white bandaging across his chest. There were bruising shadows beneath his compelling blue eyes and his hair looked as if it hadn't seen a comb for days. But to Morgen's starved gaze he was everything she'd ever wanted in a man and more.

Striving to keep her voice natural, she endeavoured to smile. 'So this is what you get up to when I leave you alone? Being an architect these days is obviously a far riskier business than I imagined it was. I'll bet you didn't have the proper footwear on. Is that why you slipped? Last time we were there the place was a quagmire.'

She knew she was babbling, but it was so good to see him up and about when she'd dreaded seeing him in a far worse scenario. Right now she was operating on pure adrenaline alone. He could have been killed, for goodness' sake!

'I'm sorry about missing our date. I didn't have your phone number on me, or I would have got someone at the hospital to ring you.' Unusually subdued, Conall stepped back to let her enter.

His sister's flat clearly had all the comforts of home, with its beautiful parquet flooring, sumptuous furniture and up-to-the-minute entertainment console, but the thought of Conall lying on that big luxurious sofa alone and in pain brought all Morgen's maternal instincts rushing to the fore.

'It doesn't matter. What matters now is that you look after yourself. Are you in pain? Did they give you something to relieve it when you got home?' She was already taking off her coat, throwing it over a chair, then turning to examine Conall more closely, her heart skipping a beat when he glanced back at her and smiled.

When Conall's gaze fell on the woman he'd been thinking about all night, the dull throbbing pain in his ribs that had robbed him of even one hour's decent rest since it happened miraculously faded as if he'd been given a wonder drug. With her long dark hair flowing loosely over her shoulders, and her green eyes wide with concern, he thought she was the most beautiful creature he had ever laid eyes on. He didn't need hospitals or painkilling drugs—all he needed was Morgen. Just being in the same room with her made everything right.

Suddenly all the loose ends in his life seemed to slot into place and find a home. The thought was exhilarating, yet terrifying. When he'd walked out on her on Sunday morning and then faced her in the office yesterday, he really thought he'd blown it. And however ready she was to forgive him now, for not showing up last night to take her to dinner because he'd had an accident, he still had his doubts about her being equally magnanimous about his earlier transgression.

'I'm doing all right, all things considered. Do you

think you could make me some coffee? The kitchen's just through there.'

'Have you eaten? I could make you some breakfast too. Why don't you go back to the sofa and lie down?'

'I don't want to lie down. I want to talk to you. I'll come in the kitchen while you make the coffee.'

Morgen found him a chair, insisting he sit while she busied herself organising coffee and toast. Every now and then she glanced anxiously at the big man cautiously holding his ribs, and her stomach would lurch in fright. Popping some bread into the toaster, she turned and leant against the counter to speak to him directly.

'So how did it happen?'

'Exactly as you said.' Shrugging his massive shoulders like a naughty schoolboy, he grimaced. 'Wrong shoes, muddy surface—then I follow the contractor up some scaffolding and lose my footing. Lucky for me I was only a few feet off the ground. If I'd been up any higher it might have been curtains.'

'That's not funny.'

'No, it isn't.' Wincing, Conall tried to make light of the fact his ribs felt as if they'd been snapped in two and tied back together again with string.

'You should never take chances like that. Where was your mind?' Realising she was scolding him because she was angry he'd been so obviously careless with his own safety, Morgen turned back to the toaster and checked the bread.

From behind, Conall said quietly, 'I was thinking about you, Morgen. I'm beginning to think you've put some kind of spell on me.'

She moved across to the fridge, found the butter she'd been looking for and brought it back to the counter.

Standing on tiptoe to reach up to a high shelf for a mug, she pretended to make light of his statement.

'Don't be silly!'

'Dammit, woman! I'm being serious!'

Her heart pounding, Morgen swung round at the reprimand. She didn't miss the wince of pain that flashed in his electric blue eyes and she was stricken with remorse.

'Please, Conall, don't get yourself all worked up. I can see that you're hurting.'

He swore softly. 'I'm hurting more because you don't seem to be taking me seriously. Just because your husband played around with your feelings doesn't mean I will do the same. I mean what I say, Morgen. I want a relationship with you...a *serious* relationship.'

A wave of shock vibrated through him. Until that moment he hadn't known himself exactly what he wanted. It seemed that walking out on Morgen on Sunday after they had slept together had changed everything. It scared Conall to see how much he might have lost with his thoughtless behaviour...might still lose if he couldn't make her see he was in earnest.

She froze. 'It wouldn't work, Conall. You're who you are, and I'm—I'm—'

'You're...?' he prompted, not bothering to mask his irritation.

'I'm a secretary who works for your firm. I'm a single mother with all the responsibility that that entails, and I can't afford to have a relationship with you. It wouldn't be fair to Neesha.'

'And what about *your* needs, Morgen? What are you saying? That you're going to remain celibate for the next fifteen years, until Neesha is old enough to leave home and have a relationship of her own?'

'Much better to do that than screw her up with lots of different men coming in and out of my life.'

'Lots of different men?' Conall rose slowly up from his seat. A muscle twitched in his jaw. 'Haven't you been listening to anything I've been saying? You seem so sure that all I want from you is a few quick tumbles in bed and that's it. I know my track record with women hasn't been the stuff of romance novels, but then I hadn't met you, had I? I never wanted to commit to anybody before because I too was cynical about relationships lasting.

'It's the old story; I saw my parents' marriage disintegrate before my eyes and was furious when they didn't patch it up and get back together—even though the break-up came about because my father couldn't resist playing around. I thought it was better to play the field a little than get serious about anyone, because I saw how broken-hearted my mother was when my father was persistently unfaithful. I was hoping to save myself from that particular pain. Unfortunately my mother just sees my non-committal attitude towards women as a character trait I've inherited from my dad. Now I see that I was wrong to treat those relationships so lightly. I probably hurt at least a couple of those women I went out with because I wouldn't commit, and I can honestly say that I regret that. They deserved better.'

He walked to the door. 'Think about it, Morgen. Next week I'm flying out to New York for a few days to wind up some business there. When I get back I'd like to know if you and I are going to get together.'

'Get together?' Her expression startled, Morgen glanced at him with troubled green eyes. 'You mean— *live* together?'

'Not straight away, but that's the general idea. I know you're concerned about the effect it will have on Neesha, but I promise you I won't be rushing anything. I'd like us both to get to know each other better first. I'd like to get to know Neesha, and to give her the chance to get to know me. Then, when a little time has passed, I'll buy us a house here in London.'

Morgen smelt burning. She spun round just as the toast popped out of the toaster and saw that it was black. Her hands shaking, she threw the burnt slices into the swing bin in the recess by her feet, then raised her gaze to Conall's again. He was leaning against the doorjamb, looking worryingly pale.

'I'll make some fresh toast. Why don't you go and lie down on the sofa and I'll bring you in a nice cup of coffee? Please, Conall. I don't think you should really be up and about at all.'

'Have you been listening to me?' Grouchy and tired, he scowled.

Morgen's heart went out to him, but even so she was wary of falling for promises that he might not be able to keep. As he admitted, his track record with women wasn't good. Why should she be the exception to the rule?

'Of course I've been listening. And I promise I'll think about what you said. But right now your health and comfort is my primary concern.'

'Shame I didn't nab a spare nurse's uniform from the hospital. Seeing you dressed up in that, with black stockings and suspenders, would do my health and comfort a power of good!' Amused at her wide-eyed reaction, as well as mildly turned on by his own outrageous fantasy, Conall turned obediently back into the living room to stretch out on the sofa.

CHAPTER TEN

BY THE time Morgen returned to the living room, with the promised coffee and toast, Conall had fallen asleep. His long jean-clad legs stuck out past the arm of the sofa, his silky brown hair flopped boyishly across his brow and his features were relaxed at last in the guise of sleep. There was an uncharacteristic vulnerability about him that brought all Morgen's nurturing instincts rushing to the fore.

Leaving the coffee and toast on a side table, she dropped down a little wearily into a nearby armchair and settled her back against two embroidered cushions. Free to pursue her own thoughts at last, she couldn't avoid the truth that was now staring her straight in the face. She was in love with Conall. Head over heels, jump through hoops, crazy about the man.

When Julie had burst into the office this morning and told her what had happened to him last night, Morgen had known then her life would never be the same if she lost him. But whether she was ready to commit to him, as he professed he was ready and willing to commit to her, Morgen still didn't know. There just seemed to be too many obstacles against their relationship working out as far as she was concerned.

Conall was used to just thinking about himself. As far as she was aware, he'd enjoyed a high-octane, fast-living life in New York and, like Simon before him, obviously moved in very different social circles from Morgen. He'd already admitted he'd dated lots of other women—and what if his mother was right? What if he was too much like his father to change? She didn't think she would be able to bear it if he were ever unfaithful to her even once—let alone several times!

And how could she risk her own and her daughter's happiness on a man who knew nothing of taking care of a family, who was unfamiliar with the demands that family made on you as well as all the mundane day-to-day domesticity that inevitably came with it? What if, after a few months, or even weeks, he started to feel trapped? Bored? The feelings he had for her would soon diminish to resentment. These things happened, and Morgen wasn't unaware of the possibility.

But oh, how she longed for him. Just knowing he was in the world made her feel better, while being with him filled her with a kind of restless excitement that wouldn't be subdued. Every cell in her body had become exquisitely sensitive to his presence, as if they were almost sharing the same breath. In bed they'd shared a passion that could light up the whole of London with its force, and Morgen had secretly basked in the power of her femininity, feeling beautiful and desired in his arms.

But what would happen when he introduced her to his friends as his former secretary? Would they look down their noses at her status? Would they think she had somehow tricked him into being with her? And what about his family? How would they react when they knew their handsome successful son had fallen for someone who worked in his office? Remembering how disdainful Simon's parents had been, Morgen shuddered. It would be a cold day in hell before she allowed anyone to make her feel so unworthy again.

Stirring in his sleep, Conall murmured something unintelligible, his sudden movement shaking Morgen out of her painful reverie. She got up, cleared away the coffee and now cold toast, and took them back into the kitchen. Plugging in the kettle, she resolved to make a cup of tea, then ring the office to see if there were any messages. As soon as Conall was awake again she would see what he needed her to do, then get back to the office just as soon as she could. If nothing else, the distance between them would maybe help her think a little straighter.

At four-thirty that afternoon, Conall rang Morgen at the office for the third time.

'Morgen?'

'Conall.' Picking up her pen, she doodled a smiley face on her shorthand pad, trying hard to ignore the fact that the sound of her racing heart was almost deafening her.

'I need you to come over here.'

'Why?' Her back straightening, her first thought was that he was in pain, or maybe needed a doctor.

'I want to see you before you go home.'

'Why?'

She heard him curse, and bit her lip to stop herself grinning.

'You ask too many questions, you know that?'

'It's part of my job. I'm trained to meet my boss's every need.'

'Now we're talking.' His voice turning gravelly, Conall chuckled down the phone. The sound had Morgen clamping her thighs together beneath her straight black skirt.

'Not *that* sort of need. Besides, you're injured. I wouldn't want to risk you hurting yourself any more than you're hurt already.'

'Sweetheart, even talking to you like this is hurting me like you can't imagine.'

Morgen imagined, and felt her body grow respondingly hot. 'If you really need to see me, I'll leave half an hour early and stop by on my way home. I can't be late tonight; I'm taking Neesha swimming.'

'I promise I won't keep you any longer than necessary. Just to see you for even five minutes would be good…and, Morgen?'

'Yes?'

'Make it soon, okay?'

'Okay.' She did another doodle of a face, and this time the smile was even wider.

There was coffee brewing when she arrived, and the delicious aroma filled the flat. Conall waited until Morgen had removed her coat, then insisted she sat down next to him on the sofa. She noticed that he'd shaved and was wearing cologne. It drifted under her nostrils every now and then, tying her senses into a straitjacket.

'Everything okay at the office?' he enquired.

Morgen nodded, trying desperately hard not to notice how long and fine his eyelashes were. 'Everything's fine. Nothing urgent to report.'

He'd obviously turned up the heating in the room, because it was almost too warm. The fact that the warmth might have more to do with Conall's well-muscled jean-clad thigh pressing up close to hers, she didn't dare dwell on. As it was, she was having trouble thinking straight around him.

'Are you still hurting?'

It was only when his blue eyes turned smokily dark that Morgen realised how easily her innocent enquiry could be misconstrued.

'Are you prepared for me to answer that?' His fingers trailed down the lapel of her jacket and slid deftly onto her silk blouse underneath, a mere half-inch from the swell of her breast.

'You've made some coffee. Shall I get us both a cup?' Jumping to her feet, Morgen escaped into the kitchen before he could answer. He followed her there, as she'd guessed he would.

'Don't you want me to touch you?' His handsome face was scowling, and there was frustration in his eyes. Morgen's blood slowed and thickened at the knowledge. Sweeping her gaze down his shirt, to the evidence of the white bandages wrapped around that wide muscular chest of his, she once again felt her heart squeeze at the idea he might really be hurting.

'Seriously, Conall, you need to be concentrating on taking care of your wounds, not worrying about whether I want you to touch me or n-not.' Blushing furiously, she turned away to pour the coffee into two mugs that were on the counter side by side in readiness. But she never got as far as reaching for the coffeepot.

Sure-footed, Conall stole up behind her, his warm breath teasing her hair. As Morgen tensed he deliberately anchored his hands either side of her hips, then nuzzled into the side of her neck with his lips. Morgen sagged against him at the contact—convinced she would surely melt into a puddle at his feet if he kept on touching her so intimately. Her limbs feeling like cooked spaghetti, she released a shaky sigh and let her head fall back against his chest.

'Ow!' His sudden groan told her he wasn't crying out in ecstasy. Mortified, she swung round to see him rue-fully shaking his head, his hand lying cautiously against his chest.

'I hurt you! Oh, Conall, I'm sorry. I should have been more careful!'

'Shut up and kiss me.'

'What?'

'You heard me.'

Careful not to pull her close into his chest, Conall captured Morgen's face between his hands, then precisely and expertly lowered his mouth to hers. He'd anticipated her taste and her heat all day, had fantasised about it stretched out on the sofa until he'd had to get up and pace the room to calm himself down. But nothing could prepare him for the blinding sensuality of their kiss. Her response astounded and aroused him, making him lean deeper into the kiss, his tongue swirling around hers, his teeth nipping at her deliciously damp plump lower lip until he was so turned on he knew he had to call a halt before events overtook him. Reluctantly he disengaged contact, ruefully putting at least three feet of chequered vinyl flooring between them.

'They should prescribe you on the National Health. I can't tell you how much better I'm feeling after that.'

Her green eyes bewildered, Morgen stared. 'Why did you stop?'

'Why did I—? Sweetheart, I want you so badly I could take you right now over the kitchen table, but I don't suppose either of us would be satisfied with that, do you?' Gratified to see her blush, and giving a silent cheer that she clearly wanted him as much as he wanted her, Conall smiled. 'Besides, you've got to get back to Neesha. I don't want you to be late for your daughter. As soon as you can next get your mother to babysit, I want you to come over and stay the night with me. Cracked ribs or no cracked ribs—it won't stop me making love to you.'

'Won't it?' Her breathing still a little laboured, and

frustration eating into her bones, Morgen couldn't disguise the longing in her eyes.

'There are always ways and means. I'll while away the lonely hours dreaming some up.'

'Okay.'

She gave him a sweet smile, and her heart swelled with joy. The fact that in the middle of their passionate embrace Conall had stopped to think about Neesha made him rise tenfold in her estimation. Maybe there was hope for a relationship between them after all? She would nurture that hope like a fledgling seed that needed water and sun to bring it to life, and for once she would try not to be cynical about the possibility of success.

'I'll pour us some coffee. What are you doing about food tonight? I don't have time to cook you anything, but I could order you a take-away.'

'I've got it covered. My mother's coming over to cook me one of her specials. What can I tell you? She loves to cook.' And would spoil him rotten if he let her. For once Conall didn't feel irked at the thought.

'She sounds like a nice woman.'

'She is. Perhaps I'll introduce you some time soon?'

Morgen guessed how that would go. She captured the thought before it ran away with her down old roads paved with heartache.

'Hmm.'

Watching him walk away back into the living room, Morgen poured the coffee and tried to convince herself that Conall's mother would be nothing like the Vaughan-Smiths.

'He seems like a very nice young man,' Lorna McKenzie said approvingly as she sat down at the table to join her daughter and granddaughter for dinner. 'I'll be happy for

Neesha to stay over Saturday night, so you can go out on a date. It'll be good for you to have some free time to yourself.'

'Nana said we can make a chocolate cake for tea. Shall I save you some, Mummy?' Glancing up from a forkful of mashed potato, Neesha's pretty face was hopeful.

'You'd better, or else there'll be big trouble! You know it's my favourite.'

'Is it Conall you're going on a date with, Mummy?' the little girl wanted to know.

Feeling both sets of eyes from across the table settle on her with great interest, Morgen glanced from Neesha to her mother and back again. 'Yes. It is Conall I'm going on a date with.'

Dinner, then back to his sister's flat in Highgate to stay the night. Her stomach clenched tight at the thought.

'Good. I'll save him some chocolate cake too.'

Morgen felt her shoulders sag with relief. At least Neesha had not put up a protest about her mother going on a date with a man, and at least she had met Conall and seemed to like him.

Early days, Morgen…one step at a time, remember? The little voice inside that was always with her warned her to proceed with caution. Just because Conall seemed perfectly serious about them seeing each other that didn't mean that they were going to have a storybook ending. In a few days' time he was going to have to make that trip of his back to New York, for closure on his business there, and a few days could be a long time when a man was back on familiar territory, with all the same temptations that had been part of his life there before.

'Eat up, Morgen. Your dinner will get cold.' From across the table Lorna McKenzie's eyes narrowed at the pensive expression on her daughter's face. He seemed like a good man, this Conall O'Brien—even if she had met him only briefly. But then Simon had seemed like a good man too, and look how wrong she had been about him.

Staring at the plans on the drawing board in front of him, Conall made a slight adjustment to an area that had been particularly bothering him. Satisfied his correction was a distinct improvement, he stood back a little to get some perspective on it. A smarting pain in the area of his right shoulder just then made him wince a little, and he rotated his arm a couple of times in a bid to ease it.

His ribs were healing nicely, if still a little sore, but it was the gash on his shoulder that seemed to cause him the most discomfort. Every time it ached he was reminded how foolish he'd been to climb that scaffolding with ordinary shoes on, and in the mud too. It really wasn't like him to be so careless, but then his thoughts had been totally preoccupied with Morgen instead of on the job in hand.

The thought of her now made him realise that he wasn't looking forward to returning to New York at all. If someone else could have gone instead of him he would have arranged it like a shot. But Conall had business there only he could sort out, as well as an apartment he rented that he needed to return the keys on, and friends he obviously needed to say goodbye to. He'd already decided that when Derek Holden was back in the fray—providing, of course, that he'd got a grip on his addiction to drink—he was going to send him out to the New York office and a new life. It was probably just the challenge the man needed. At least it would help take his mind off all the problems he'd had at home.

And as soon as he himself got back from the States he

was going to look seriously into buying a house—a house he hoped that eventually Morgen and Neesha would come to share with him. But first he had to convince the lady that he was in earnest.

'Conall?'

Suddenly she was there, and Conall felt the ache in his shoulder miraculously recede.

'Come in and shut the door.'

'I only wanted to leave these letters with you to sign.' Her expression unsure, she hovered in the doorway, feeling suddenly ridiculously shy around him.

'Come in anyway. I want to talk.'

Finding herself waved into the comfy leather chair opposite Conall's desk, Morgen laid her hands in her lap and waited. To put her at ease, Conall decided to start off with a neutral subject.

'I've spoken to Derek at the clinic. I just wanted to let you know that he's doing fine. He had a few shaky days to start with, but apparently he's now determined to kick the booze and get back on track with his life.'

'That's great news!' Her pretty green eyes alight with pleasure, Morgen leaned happily towards the big man in the chair opposite. 'I knew he could do it!'

'It's early days yet, sweetheart. He's got four more weeks at the clinic, then we'll see—yes?'

'I don't doubt for a minute that he can do it.' More subdued, Morgen leant back in her seat. 'I know you probably saw him at his worst, but he's not the hopeless case you might think he is.'

'I never believed his case was hopeless, but addiction is a disease. Some can beat it; some can't.'

'Anyway, it's the best news. Thanks for telling me.'

Picking up a ballpoint pen from the blotter in front of him, Conall twirled it thoughtfully between his fingers.

'What would you say if I told you he probably wasn't coming back here to work?'

'Why?'

'Because I'm thinking of sending him to the New York office. A change of scene would most likely do him the power of good. New people, new challenges, a new life.'

'I can see how that might work,' Morgen agreed. 'Though I'll miss him, of course.'

'You'll be working for me instead.' His expression brooding, Conall directed his gaze straight at her. He saw the brief flicker of doubt in her eyes and couldn't prevent the sudden knot in his stomach. Did the prospect really bother her that much?

'Because I'm the head of the firm it will be a promotion, of course. More responsibility and more money...how does that sound?'

Under any other circumstances it would have sounded good, Morgen decided. But with her promise to both her mother and Neesha to somehow cut down her working hours so that she could spend more time with her daughter it was really the last thing she needed to hear. Not to mention the fact that she now had a highly personal relationship with Conall that she didn't feel was particularly conducive to their professional one.

It would only be a matter of time before the whole office found out that something was going on between Derek Holden's PA and Conall O'Brien. Potentially it could cause a great deal of resentment and make life even more difficult for her.

'I've been meaning to talk to you about this.'

'What, specifically?'

'Our working together.' Shifting uncomfortably in her seat, Morgen fiddled with a strand of her hair, then, leaving it alone, glanced directly at Conall. 'You must see that it wouldn't work on a permanent basis. Not when we're—we're seeing each other socially. Plus there's the fact that I was going to talk to you about the possibility of cutting down my hours anyway. I need to be there more for Neesha. I've been working full-time since she was a baby. She's growing up so fast, and I'll never have this time back. I've already missed things in her life that I won't get the opportunity of enjoying again. So, thanks for thinking of me, but I really think, all things considered, that you ought to give the job to someone else.'

Glowering, Conall got to his feet. 'Nobody else knows the work as well as you! I had that bubble-headed Julie working for me for those few days you were off sick, and she's an okay PA, but ask the woman to think on her feet and she dissolves into a puddle of girlish incompetence that just brings out the caveman in me!'

To her shock, Morgen burst out laughing. Green eyes brimming with mirth, she clutched her stomach to stop it from hurting. 'And you *don't* act the caveman with me?'

He frowned and sat down again, blue eyes troubled. 'Are you saying I'm difficult to work with?'

'No.' Morgen's voice was firm. 'I'm not saying that at all. I'm saying that if you're serious about us having a personal relationship then I can't work for you as well. You know it makes sense.'

'Trust me to find a woman who's got scruples as well as standards I can't help but admire.' He smiled then, and it was like standing in a pool of sunshine after a grey cloud had passed.

'So you'll look for someone else to fill the post?'

'Not until the next few weeks are up—until I see how Derek's doing. Then I'll give you my verdict. In the meantime I think we should look at how we can shorten your hours. I can see that it's important for you to spend more time with Neesha.'

'Thank you.' Expelling a long sigh of relief, Morgen got up from her chair to leave.

'Where are you going?' Conall demanded.

'I've got work to do.'

He stood up and came round the desk, a glint in his eye that Morgen was beginning to recognise.

'Not until you kiss me first.'

'Conall! Someone might walk in—'

He strode to the door, twisted the catch and locked it. A sexy grin making him look exceedingly wicked, he returned to a gaping-mouthed Morgen and grasped her firmly by the arms. 'Not now, they won't!'

CHAPTER ELEVEN

IT WAS raining when they came out of the restaurant late on Saturday—not heavily, but a slow driving drizzle that made Morgen's dark hair look as if it was shrouded in a filmy net. Slipping his hand beneath her elbow, Conall jogged her to the car, opening the passenger door first to let her get comfortable before sliding in next to her in the driver's seat.

'You okay?' His blue eyes flashed concern as she pulled the collar of her coat up more securely round her ears. It was a particularly chilly evening, and as well as the rain the wind was raw.

'I'm fine. I'll soon warm up.'

All evening he'd gazed his fill of her, but it never seemed to be quite enough. They'd talked, sometimes skirting round more personal subjects to make polite chit-chat, both knowing there was a conversation of a more meaningful kind going on elsewhere in their minds and in their bodies.

In the flat, Conall had adjusted the lighting to low. The softer light welcomed them in from the cold, creating an atmosphere of warmth and intimacy, sending shivers of delicious anticipation scurrying down Morgen's spine. It was scary to want him so much, to need him. It had been a long time since she'd allowed herself to need a man, and Simon hadn't really needed her at all in the way she'd needed him. But Conall was different. They had a *connection*. It was stupid to deny it any longer.

Back at the restaurant Morgen had hardly been able to

do justice to their wonderful meal, because every time their glances had met a small firework display seemed to go off in her stomach, and two glasses of wine had consequently gone straight to her head. Now, as she slipped off her coat and handed it to him, she was alarmed to find that her legs were shaking, as if she'd just got off the Twister at the fairground.

Catching her shiver, Conall hesitated before taking care of her coat. 'Still cold?'

'No. It's lovely and warm in here.'

'Sit down. Make yourself comfortable. I'll get us both a drink.'

'No more alcohol, please.' Her smile was apologetic. 'More than two glasses of wine and I'll flake out for the night.'

'I'm glad you warned me.' His voice deeply sexy in timbre, he smiled in a way that lowered her resistance to zero and made her forget to breathe. On his way to the kitchen he arranged her coat and his jacket on the back of a large comfy armchair and asked her if she'd prefer coffee instead.

'Lovely.' Rubbing her arms in the blue and white silk dress she wore, Morgen dropped down onto the sofa and kicked off her shoes. Curling her stockinged toes into the deeply luxurious carpet, she gazed round at the various prints on the pale-coloured walls, peered closer at the family photographs lining the pine mantel, then allowed her gaze to wander over the eclectic *objets d'art* arranged on shelves and bookcases. Everything was tasteful and beautiful, but obviously said a lot more about Conall's sister than they did about him.

'Why don't you have a place of your own?'

On impulse, her feet took her into the kitchen, where Conall was arranging cups and saucers on a tray, then pouring sugar from a cellophane packet into a little porcelain bowl. He appeared quite at home with the ordinary domestic tasks, and Morgen was equally content just to watch him. That broad back of his was like an artist's model's, with the suggestion of muscle rippling gently beneath his shirt every time he moved, and her eyes dipped appreciatively to his taut lean behind and those long, long legs in smart tailored trousers.

'I was renting an apartment in Chelsea up until I left for New York. To be frank, I never really felt the need to have somewhere permanent. The last few years I've been travelling a lot: America, Canada, Australia—what was the point in having a place that would be empty most of the time?'

'And now that you've decided to stay in the UK for a while?'

He stopped what he was doing, turning round to lean against the counter, his electric blue eyes a stunning contrast to the whiteness of his shirt. 'I'm thinking about buying a house.'

'Not designing one?' Morgen knew that if she had the enviable skills Conall possessed she would love to design a house of her own.

'The thought had crossed my mind.'

Before she had time to think Conall was standing in front of her, running his hands up her bare arms in her silk dress, drowning her senses in his potently virile, not-to-be-ignored maleness. 'But it depends on whether or not I've got somebody special to share it with me.'

'You'll find someone.' Tearing her gaze away from the sensual hunger simmering in his, Morgen focused instead on the little pearlescent buttons on his shirt.

'I thought I already had.'

'You might want to think again.' Her voice low,

Morgen dragged her gaze back up to his, her heartbeat faltering and stumbling at the sheer masculine beauty of his face. 'I've got a daughter, remember? This isn't just about you and me. Have you any idea what it's like to be responsible for a child? You're used to being free and single, coming and going as you please. You can't do that when you have children. Your whole focus is on them, and you never stop worrying about them. That's what you'd be taking on, Conall, and somehow—' She broke away from him to stand in the doorway. 'Somehow I don't think you're ready for that.'

Taken by surprise, Conall was momentarily silenced. *Children...* He'd honestly not dedicated a lot of thought to being a father. Up until now he'd always relegated that possibility to the dim and distant future, convinced that when and if that time ever came he would be mature enough to handle it...unlike his own father.

Having Morgen and Neesha in his life would completely change the way he lived. He'd never even flat-shared before, let alone lived with a woman. There were a lot of new things he would have to get used to, but they weren't exactly things he *dreaded*, he found. It might be sort of nice, having two females about the place. And being able to wake up next to the woman of his dreams each morning was an incentive he couldn't ignore. No. Morgen was wrong about him. He was far more adaptable than she thought. If he wasn't, he wouldn't have decided to transfer back to the UK at the drop of a hat all because he was in love with someone, would he?

In love... The thought swirled over him like a mist, shrouding him in wonder. He felt excited, enthused. His heart stumbling over itself to get a rhythm, he smiled.

In the arsenal of advantages he already possessed, that

smile of his was the most explosive weapon of all, Morgen decided.

'You're wrong about me, Morgen. I want you and Neesha in my life. I want to take care of you both. I may not know much about taking care of kids, but I've always been quick to catch on, and I can learn as I go along, can't I? I won't let you down. If you think this is some kind of temporary whim on my part, then you really don't know me at all. I've never fallen for a woman so hard before.'

Urging Morgen away from the door, he captured her face between his hands. 'What do you say to us getting married?'

If a bomb had ripped through the ceiling just then Morgen couldn't have been more shocked. Dizzy for a moment, she glanced up into Conall's smiling blue eyes and lost the power of speech. *Marriage?* It wasn't something that she had imagined he would ever consider for one second. When he'd talked of buying a house, and sharing it with her and Neesha, Morgen had assumed he meant her to cohabit with him.

Sliding her hands up to cover his, she gently pulled them away. 'We've only known each other such a short time. We shouldn't rush into anything we might regret. I know you're probably thinking of me, but we don't have to get married in order to be together. I'll think about moving in with you eventually, but I really need more time.'

It wasn't the answer Conall wanted to hear. He'd astounded himself with his offer of marriage, and it hadn't been until the words were out of his mouth that he'd realised it was what he desired above all else. As far as he was concerned he'd found the person he wanted to share the rest of his life with, and he wasn't about to let her get away.

'I asked you to marry me because I'm in love with you, Morgen.'

Morgen bit her lip. 'Simon said he loved me too. Words like that come easy at the beginning of an affair, and you've already admitted your track record isn't good.'

Stunned, Conall cursed harshly beneath his breath and stepped away. 'So I'm to get no opportunity to redeem myself? It wasn't as if I hid anything from you about my past. I admitted I've never wanted to commit to anyone before, but I deeply resent being compared to your ex-husband. Can't you see that this is different?'

Morgen wanted to believe him, but she'd lost the ability to trust when Simon had walked out on her. How could she explain to Conall that she'd been absolutely terrified to find herself falling for him? That she couldn't help drawing comparisons with her relationship with Simon because when he'd walked out on her she'd hardly believed she would recover from such rejection. With his parents' disdain of her background, Morgen had lost all sense of self-esteem and worth. What if Conall's family treated her similarly?

'You saw where I live, Conall. You know I don't move in the same social circles as you, with monied, professional people. What are your friends going to think when they find out you've fallen for an ordinary secretary from South London, and a single mother to boot?'

'I can't believe any of this would even bother you! Yes, I've seen where you live, and what I saw was a home—not an empty shell fitted out with designer furniture, but a real home. Something I haven't had since I was a kid. And though it might be true to say that some of my friends inhabit the kind of social circles you hint at, and in the past I've been guilty of using my wealth and connections to my advantage, I personally don't give a damn about any of that stuff any more! I take people as I find them—no matter where they're from or what they do. I either like them or I don't, and the ones I don't like I leave well alone.'

Striding to the counter, he turned on a tap and splashed water into a glass tumbler. Taking a long drink, he turned back to broodingly consider Morgen on the other side of the kitchen.

'And for your information I don't give a damn what people think either way. This is you and me we're talking about. Either you want to be with me or you don't. When you get right down to it, that's the only thing that matters.'

Sucking in a deep breath, Morgen released it slowly. 'I do want to be with you,' she confessed quietly. 'Okay. I'll really think seriously about moving in with you, but I won't marry you.'

Meeting her gaze and recognising the hint of steel in the depths of soft green, Conall felt his chest constrict with deep disappointment and hurt. The first woman he'd ever asked to marry him and she'd turned him down. To say it wasn't a blow to his pride and his manhood would be a huge lie. Returning the glass of water to the counter, he slowly folded his arms across his chest.

'If you won't agree to marry me then I won't ask you to move in with me.'

'That's up to you.' Hot colour shading her cheekbones, and a brief flash of disbelief in her eyes, Morgen turned and walked away.

* * *

'I want you to phone that number and book me on a morning flight to New York tomorrow.'

Staring down at the sheet of paper Conall had slapped down on her desk, Morgen swallowed hard. Saturday hadn't turned out at all as they'd planned. After telling him she wasn't going to marry him things had gone steadily downhill. Instead of ending up in bed together, as both had eagerly anticipated, Morgen had found herself asking him to ring her a cab to take her home. Refusing to do any such thing, he'd insisted instead on driving her home himself.

To say the atmosphere between them had deteriorated to a morose silence simply didn't equate with the harsh reality. When he'd bade her goodbye at her door he hadn't even hesitated before striding away down the street back to his car. Morgen had let herself into a cold and lonely house, her mind numb, without even the companionship of her little daughter to help ease her heartache.

'I'll see to it right away.'

'I'll be gone for most of the week. If anything important comes up ring me direct. I've left you my home number as well.'

'Okay.'

Finally she allowed her gaze to lock with his. The anger she saw simmering there, reminding her of hot springs, made her catch her breath. She didn't want it to be like this between them, but how was she going to make things right? Marriage terrified her. Her divorce from Simon had been messy and acrimonious, and she'd vowed to never repeat the experience. She'd had to fight to get any support at all for her child. The thought of marrying Conall only for their union to end in bitter divorce was her worst nightmare. She couldn't do it, and she wouldn't want to make him ever regret knowing her.

'And I've got Richard Akers coming in for a one o'clock meeting. Organise some refreshments, will you?'

She nodded mutely, hating the terse, formal way he was addressing her. Was it going to be like this from now on, until she stopped working for him?

'I'll see to it.'

'I've no doubt you will, Morgen. You're nothing if not professional at your job.'

Before she had even a hope of unravelling his meaning his door had shut, leaving her staring at her computer screen as though she was in a trance.

He was staring out of the window again, his concentration shattered, his fury growing steadily by the minute. Why wouldn't she marry him? The way she'd acted when he'd asked, anyone would think he'd insulted her! She obviously didn't believe he was serious. What the hell had her ex done to her to make her so untrusting? The thought made Conall's gut clench. And what was all that about him moving in different social circles from her? He'd spent the whole of Saturday night and most of Sunday trying to fathom out why she seemed so perturbed about it. The fact was, he should have sat down and talked with her more. Instead he'd let his hurt and rejection—not to mention his anger—get the better of him, behaved like a sulky child who hadn't been able to get his own way. No wonder she'd wanted to go home in preference to sharing his bed!

That thought alone undid him. He'd been walking around as though the ground was covered in tin-tacks since he'd driven her home, sexual frustration almost making him lose his mind. Dammit, he couldn't even look at her without being so turned on it hurt. In contrast, when she turned those damnably soft wary green eyes of hers on him, she made him feel like the man who'd shot Bambi's mother. How to repair the damage before he took off to New York tomorrow? If he didn't at least try he'd spend the better part of a week being impossible to work with. It was a dead certainty his colleagues wouldn't appreciate the fact.

The buzzer sounded on his telephone. Irritably Conall barked into it. 'Yes!'

'I've got Victoria Kendall in Reception, asking to see you. Shall I bring her in?'

What the hell was his mother doing at the office? Drumming his fingers impatiently on the desk, Conall let loose a groan.

'All right. Go and get her.'

In the outer office, Morgen smoothed down her black skirt with nervous hands, straightened her jacket, glanced perfunctorily in the mirror on the wall above the filing cabinet, then walked with what she hoped was a confident air along the corridor and out into the plush reception area.

'Ms Kendall? I'm Morgen McKenzie—Mr O'Brien's assistant. If you'd like to come with me, I'll take you to him.'

Impeccably dressed, with light brown hair and blue eyes as dazzling as her son's, Victoria Kendall shook the younger woman's hand with a smile, then followed her into the corridor.

'I expect he's not best pleased to see me,' she confided chattily to a surprised Morgen. 'He probably thinks I'm going to give him another lecture, when all I want to do is take him to lunch. He hasn't got anything important booked, has he? I know I probably should have rung first but—well, I was in town and sort of acted on impulse.'

Immediately Morgen felt herself warm to this woman. Unexpectedly maternal, despite her glamorous appearance, Victoria Kendall was not what she'd anticipated she'd be. In contrast, Simon's mother had been so cold—supermarket freezers were warmer.

'He does have a one o'clock meeting, but I'm sure he could postpone it until later.'

Now, why had she said that? Conall—not to mention the pompous, self-important Richard Akers—would likely kill her.

'Well, that certainly sounds hopeful! Thank you, my dear.'

To Morgen's shock, Conall was waiting in the outer office, his pacing feet wearing a hole in the carpet as they entered.

'What's the problem, Mother? You know I'm busy.'

'What a greeting! I think I'll turn around and go home again.' Her expression offended, Victoria started to move back towards the door.

Appalled by his rudeness, Morgen jumped swiftly to the older woman's defence. 'Your mother came to invite you to lunch, Conall, and I really think you should go. I can easily postpone your meeting with Richard Akers until later on this afternoon.'

'Why should I do that? And who asked your opinion anyway? You know damn well I'm flying out to New York tomorrow, and I'm up to my ears in work!'

'Conall O'Brien! Since when did you forget the manners I raised you with?' Marching up to her tall, broad-shouldered giant of a son, Victoria stood in front of him and glared. 'Now, I want you to apologise to your secretary immediately! It's perfectly true I came to take you to lunch. She was only speaking up on my behalf.'

'I'm sorry, but the fact of the matter is I'm still too

busy to go to lunch with you, Mother. Why don't you let Morgen make you a cup of tea, and just relax for a few minutes before you set off home again?'

'Was that an apology? Did I miss something?' Victoria frowned at Conall, then at Morgen.

The exceptionally pretty young woman with the glossy dark hair had gone quite pink in the cheeks, she noticed. Also, her hands trembled slightly as she picked up some papers off the desk and shuffled them back into order. Interesting. Was this the woman her son had fallen for? She could easily see why. Her frown was quickly replaced by a dazzling smile that could only be matched by one of her son's.

'Even if you're madly busy there is never any call for rudeness,' she lightly scolded Conall. 'But if you really don't want me to treat you to lunch, perhaps Morgen would like to join me for a cup of tea and a chat instead? You can spare her for a little while, can't you?'

Like a police dog on the scent of a criminal, Conall wrinkled his brow in suspicion. 'Now, why on earth would you want to chat to my secretary?' he demanded irritably.

What could you possibly have in common with her? Morgen finished for him in her head.

That did it for her—that note of insulting disdain that had crept into his voice. It was the straw that broke the camel's back, as far as she was concerned. Throwing the sheaf of papers she had so carefully reassembled furiously down on the desk, so that they scattered everywhere, she turned to Conall with spitting green eyes, her chest heaving with the force of her anger at his insufferable condescension.

'Does making people feel small come naturally to you, or did you take lessons? Well, for your information, *Mr*

O'Brien, I've put up with your bad temper and ill manners all morning, and I'm not going to put up with them for a moment longer! See how well you can manage when I take the afternoon off!'

'Now, wait just a minute, here. I—'

She heard the fury in his voice and, grabbing up her bag, headed out of the door as fast as her legs would carry her. Not really knowing where she intended to go, she pushed open a nearby door as she heard him hurry after her, slipped inside and firmly locked it shut behind her. Inside the small dark room that housed the firm's stationery, Morgen tugged on a slim cord dangling from the ceiling and hefted a relieved sigh when the light came on.

'Morgen!'

Outside the room, Conall rattled the metal door handle back and forth. 'What the hell do you think you're playing at?'

'Stop bullying me! I don't want to talk to you. You can have my notice on your desk in the morning!'

In the silence that followed, the only sound she could hear was the thundering of her heart. A lone tear slid down her cheek, but she impatiently brushed it away. She wouldn't let him treat her like some kind of brainless minion! She just wouldn't! That had been Simon's trick, and Morgen was damned if she was going to let Conall replicate it.

'I'm flying to New York in the morning, remember?' The timbre of his voice was a low growl laced with pure frustration.

'So you are,' Morgen snapped. 'I hope you stay there and never come back!'

'You don't mean that.' He rattled the door handle one more time. 'Let me come in and talk to you.'

'I don't want to talk to you. There's nothing more to be said.'

'There's plenty to be said! Open the door, Morgen, and let me in. Please!'

Hitching her shoulder bag more firmly onto her shoulder, she settled her fingers warily round the key in the lock. 'I'll open the door, but I'm not going to talk to you, Conall, so don't think I am. As a matter of fact, I'm going straight home.'

His height and breadth of chest immediately swamped her as she turned the handle, and to her complete shock Morgen found herself hustled back into the tiny little room, with Conall glaring down at her and the door unceremoniously kicked shut behind him. All of a sudden her senses were completely overpowered by his maleness, and she backed up against some hardwood shelves, her breathing shallow and uneven. She could see the glint of sweat on his brow, and his face looked hard and unyielding in the harsh orange light of the room.

'What—what do you think you're doing?'

'I'm not moving from here until you talk to me.'

'Your mother's waiting in the office. Go back to her. I'll go for a walk and come back in an hour. I won't really hand in my notice. You know I need this job, and I—'

'What are you so frightened of, Morgen?' The sudden gentling in his tone caught her off guard. Biting her lip to stop herself from crying, Morgen exhaled a shuddering sigh.

'I'm not—I just don't want to talk about this. And I— I don't like the way you spoke to me in there…like— like I was somehow beneath you. Please move out of my way so I can go.'

'I'm sorry if that's how I made you feel.' He grimaced.

'I just let my frustration get the better of me. I didn't mean anything by it. Now, please answer my question. What are you so frightened of? I'm staying right where I am until you tell me.'

Everything about him was implacable. Like a hard granite wall that even a wrecking ball would have trouble dismantling. Morgen stole an anxious glance at his intense blue eyes and swallowed to try and ease the ache in her throat.

'I'm frightened of my feelings for you, if you must know! I don't want to want you so much, but I do. It makes me afraid, Conall. You're used to being in charge, giving orders. You're at the peak of your career—wealthy and successful. I was married to a man who had those attributes too, but he thought that made him so much better than me. Because he was a doctor and I was *just* a secretary. He belittled where I came from, where I'd gone to school—what my parents did for a living. He even thought he was better than our baby! His parents turned their backs on Neesha, do you know that? Their own grandchild! By the time our marriage ended I didn't have such a good opinion about myself. I don't ever want to feel like that again. Can you understand?'

At last, Conall could. Seeing tears glistening in her beautiful eyes made his chest hurt. Reaching out, he touched her face, stroked away the moisture on her delicately soft cheek, then dropped a butterfly kiss on her softly parted mouth.

'If I've ever made you feel less than you should, then I'm mortally sorry. I've always thought of you as my equal in every way. You put other women in the shade—you know that? With your beauty, your wit, your intelligence, the way you take care of your child. You're a remarkable person, Morgen. That's why I want you to be my wife.'

CHAPTER TWELVE

A LOUD rapping on the door startled them both.

'Hold that thought.' Smiling wryly, Conall bit back his obvious frustration.

'Conall? Are you in there with Morgen? Why don't you both come back into the office and I'll make you some coffee?'

'Mother.' Ruefully shaking his head, Conall tugged gently at Morgen's hand. 'She won't go away until she gets to the bottom of this, you know. She's not known in the family as "Columbo" for nothing. We'd better go back. I'm sorry if I've been like a bear with a sore head this morning. I had no right to take things out on you.'

Hardly trusting herself to speak, Morgen risked a brief wobbly smile.

'Apology accepted.'

'Do you have a photograph of Neesha I might see?' Sitting beside Morgen's desk, her hands curled around a steaming mug of coffee with a liberal helping of sugar, Victoria Kendall leaned forward with interest as Morgen delved into her bag.

When it came to her little girl—her pride and joy—Morgen had no trouble in producing pictures on request. She had a generous selection in her wallet that she always carried around with her. The fact that Conall's mother professed to be genuinely interested in her child and didn't seem in any hurry to leave made the younger woman warm to her even more.

'Oh, she's beautiful!' Victoria exclaimed, glancing up as Conall came back into the room. Smiling, he went behind his mother's chair and peered over her shoulder at the colour photograph in her hand.

'Just like her mother,' he remarked.

The comment tugged powerfully at Morgen's heart and made her feel as if she was suddenly falling into space. Her gaze touched Conall's and a burst of warmth exploded inside her.

Noticing the longing in that glance in her son's direction, Victoria Kendall smiled inwardly with a feeling of great satisfaction. She'd waited a long time for her handsome son to fall in love, and right now, studying the lovely brunette who sat before her, wearing her heart in her eyes, she prayed he really had found the one. His soul mate.

The only thing that slightly perturbed Victoria was that she sensed Morgen might need some little persuasion in the right direction. Being a single mum, she was obviously concerned for the wellbeing of her child, and wouldn't want to rush into anything unless she was absolutely sure that Conall was one hundred per cent committed to them both. No doubt Conall's reputation with the ladies had preceded him, and it was understandable that Morgen should be a little reticent under the circumstances. But Conall wasn't really a carbon copy of his father. He might have enjoyed the ladies, but he hadn't made any promises he couldn't keep, and Victoria had always felt in her heart that when he eventually found the right woman he would stay completely loyal to her.

When he made up his mind about something he stuck to it, and Victoria didn't doubt that her son would stick by Morgen through thick and thin. Therefore she resolved

to do all that she could to help matters along to a satis-
factory conclusion. What mother worth her salt wouldn't?

Handing Neesha's picture back to her, Victoria reached
up and slid her hand across Conall's. 'It's not too late to
take Morgen to lunch, you know, darling.'

Shaking his head with genuine regret, Conall sighed.
'It's a nice idea, Mother, but I really, honestly cannot
spare the time. When I get back from New York, in a
few days' time, I promise the first thing I'll do is take
Morgen out to lunch. Does that make you feel better?'

'I know you'll do the right thing, son.' Confidently,
Victoria smiled.

Morgen worked her socks off to make sure Conall left a
clean slate when he went to New York. At half past six
that same evening she finally switched off her computer,
slipped on her jacket, from where it had hung on the back
of her chair, stood up and stretched her arms wide.
Glancing nervously at the light showing under his door,
she patted her hand against her mouth to capture a yawn,
then stood there wondering what to do next.

She was going to have to go in and tell him she was
going home. It wouldn't be easy, knowing she wasn't
going to see him for at least the next four days, maybe
more. The ache in her heart was deep and irrevocable—
like a physical pain. Why hadn't she given him an answer
when he'd said he wanted her to be his wife earlier? He'd
asked her to 'hold that thought', but would he think because she hadn't brought the subject up again she still
wasn't interested? As far as she was concerned he had
given her the assurance she sought. He didn't care where
she lived or what her background was; he'd told her he
thought of her as his equal.

Oh, God…please don't let him change his mind.

*   *   *

Pinching the bridge of his nose, then rubbing the tiredness away from his eyes, Conall welcomed the distraction the knock on the door brought. Feeling a little frisson of heat zigzag through his body when he saw who his visitor was, he rose from his seat, yanked off his expensive silk tie and threw it carelessly onto the desk.

'I just came to tell you that I'm going home now.'

Her tentative smile slipped away from her lips, as if she was unsure about letting her guard down. The brief tantalising glimpse seduced Conall's already aroused senses like satin sheets against bare skin, and anticipation seeped into his blood and quietly simmered. Dropping his gaze to the vee of her blouse beneath her opened jacket, and the pink cotton that lovingly caressed her comely curves, he felt heat explode inside him, obliterating any last vestiges of fatigue he might be feeling.

'Come in and shut the door,' he told her.

She didn't protest, as he'd thought she might. Having done what he asked, Morgen moved towards him, carefully looping her hair behind her ear, her interested glance on the architectural plans spread out before him on the desk, the blue of his silk tie a vivid splash of colour against the black and white of the drawings.

'Not finished yet?' she asked.

'Sweetheart, I've done all I'm going to do for tonight.' Without further ado Conall rescued his tie, pushed it deep into his trouser pocket, then rolled up the drawings and stashed them by the filing cabinet behind him. His desk clear, he let loose a heartstopping grin that knocked her sideways.

'Anyway, I hope you have a good trip. I'll keep you posted if anything important comes up.'

'Ever the efficient assistant.'

'I try to do my best.'

'I wish you'd said you aim to please.'

'I do.' Puzzled at his meaning, Morgen self-consciously tugged the sides of her jacket across her blouse.

'Then if that's true, please don't do that.'

'What?'

His blue eyes slumberously dark, as if he had just woken from the most languid sleep, Conall rocked her world with the shocking sensuality of his hot direct glance.

'Hide your body from me.'

'I'm…I'm not.' Dropping her hands to her sides, Morgen dragged her gaze away from his before she went up in flames. All of a sudden her limbs felt curiously slow and heavy, as if she was in one of those dreams where she wanted to run but couldn't. Only this time she had no intention of running. Forcing herself to look at Conall again, she unwittingly moistened her lips with her tongue.

For Conall, on the receiving end of that innocently erotic little gesture, desire was swift and merciless in its retribution. All his muscles bunched in an effort to maintain control.

'I need you to take something down for me, Miss McKenzie.' There was a husky catch in his voice that completely undid Morgen.

'I thought you'd finished for the night…Mr O'Brien.'

'There's something I've been wanting to do all day. Do you mind?'

She moved slowly round to where he stood, and her breath stalled in her lungs when he guided her gently back onto the desk, then slipped off her shoes. His touch was warm and sure, and Morgen felt like a cat stretched out on a window ledge, waiting for the sun to come up and caress her with its rays.

Truth to tell, she'd been wanting this all day too. It had been torment to watch him go about his business without being able to touch him. Ever the cool, polished professional, his slightly aloof office persona had tantalised her, playing on her nerves until she'd thought she might scream if she didn't get some relief soon. Now there was no intention whatsoever in her mind to deny herself this sublime intoxication of the senses. She had been craving nothing else since he had stormed into her life, accusing her of not doing her job properly.

Though her natural inclination was to wrap her arms around his waist, he moved his head, indicating that she stay where she was, smiled wickedly, then eased down her pantyhose and underwear with a shockingly erotic artistry that made her head spin. She was immediately damp and flushed. A wave of love consumed her, and carried her along on its crest.

'You're wearing too many clothes,' he scolded softly, but before Morgen's fingers could get to her blouse buttons he captured her hand, the corners of his mouth hitching up in one of the sexiest traffic-stopping smiles known to woman. 'Let me.'

Pushing aside the freed material, his mouth captured a breast beneath the thin silk of her lacy black bra, his heat scalding her nipple, making it surge into a tight peak and shamelessly arch towards him for more. Knowing what she needed, what she craved, he moved to her other breast to lavish the same treatment. The connection deep inside Morgen's womb was electrifying.

Excitement consuming her, she gasped as his hand slid up the inside of her thigh, stroking and kneading the soft smooth flesh he found there, while Morgen drove her fingers through the thick short strands of his hair and hungrily sought his mouth. When their lips met, hotly, desperately, passion ignited like an inferno, leaving them gasping and trembling in its wake.

'Conall, please.'

'What is it, Miss McKenzie?' he teased, his voice a low, hungry rasp against her ear.

'You know.' Twisting her head, she claimed his mouth in another mind-blowing kiss, her tongue sliding in and out of his sensual heat, feeling the rasp of his unshaven jaw abrade the sensitive skin on her chin, her cheek—his male scent invading her everywhere so that her own body felt like a living extension of his.

'Tell me.'

'Love me...please love me.'

He gazed into eyes that reminded him of melting mint-green ice, framed with velvet black lashes. Her lush pink mouth was damp and slightly pouting from the passion of their kisses, and every other woman he'd ever felt desire for melted into oblivion, as though they'd never existed. On fire for her practically since the moment she'd walked into the room, Conall was inside her before he had his next thought. Her heat surrounding him, he felt her muscles flex and contract around him, all his desire, all his simmering frustration and longing for her finally crowning in his deep and voracious possession.

Guiding her hips towards him, then burying her face in the hard strength of his massive chest, Morgen gladly accepted his passionate, urgent thrusts, her heartbeat galloping in her breast, the need in her spiralling swiftly into such profound tension that something had to give soon. It did. The walls of her muscles contracting almost violently around him, she gasped aloud, her nails biting into his back beneath the thin material of his shirt as one final thrust resulted in his own powerful climax and his liquid heat spilling deep into her womb.

Overcome by their profound connection, Morgen lifted her head to gaze, stunned, into his eyes. The love she saw reflected there amazed and astounded her. Reaching up, she pressed a tender lover's kiss on the side of his mouth, then another, then another. Still locked together, her skirt up around her waist and her legs around Conall's hips, Morgen allowed herself to fully experience the sense of delicious wickedness that had invaded her for a little while longer. They'd made love…on Derek's desk, for goodness' sake! She'd never be able to look at that desk again without remembering.

'Have I told you how gorgeous I think you are, Miss McKenzie?' His hand sliding between them onto her milk-smooth white breast, Conall rubbed and squeezed her nipple inside her bra, making Morgen feel that heavy drugging sensation in her limbs all over again.

'As a matter of fact, I don't think you have.'

'Well, you are—and I'm crazy about you. That's why I want to marry you.'

Before she realised what he intended, he'd reached round to her back, tugged her blouse out of her skirt and unhooked her bra. Her breasts spilled freely and unashamedly into his hands as he shoved the material out of the way and lowered his mouth to each one in turn.

'What about living for the—the moment…hmm?'

But her barely gasped words were stolen away by what he was doing to her body. Tipping back her head, Morgen was swept away by the fierce ache that ruthlessly took hold of her, determined to give Conall loving like he'd never known before, so that there wouldn't be one single minute while he was in New York that he wouldn't think of her and long to be home.

*   *   *

'What's this? You doing a little freelancing on the side, Con?'

Mike Brabourn, fellow architect and friend, directed a trained eye over the plans on Conall's desk, then waited interestedly for his reply.

'You could say that.'

Inexplicably irked by his friend's curiosity, Conall swiftly rolled up the plans and slid them expertly back into their cardboard tube. Picking up a pen, he tapped it on the blotter in front of him.

Mike frowned. 'So what gives? You still haven't told me the real reason you're relocating back to England—and don't try to pull the wool over my eyes either. I know when you're being economical with the truth—I've known you too long, remember?'

Conall remembered. He hadn't shared the news that he'd fallen in love and planned to get married with anyone but Victoria—and even she didn't know about the marriage part yet. He didn't feel it was right, telling her his intentions when he still hadn't had a proper answer from Morgen. They'd had never-to-be-forgotten sex on the desk in his office, but he still hadn't got her to agree to marry him. She'd tantalised him with the promise that as soon as he got back from New York he could have his answer.

So far, Conall had endured three agonisingly sleepless nights, wondering if she was going to turn him down after all. The traffic noise of one of the busiest cities in the world hadn't helped either. He'd found himself lying awake in his plush high-rise apartment, dreaming of a place of his own in the English countryside, with Morgen and Neesha and maybe a puppy for Neesha to play with. The idea had made his imagination catch fire, and finally he'd been motivated enough to get up in the middle of the night and sketch out some plans for a house he suddenly wanted to build...

'Conall?' Mike waved a hand in front of his face, then stopped abruptly. 'The penny's just dropped. It's a woman, isn't it? You've gone and fallen for someone, haven't you?'

Pushing to his feet, Conall dropped his hands to his hips and grinned. 'Is it so obvious?'

'What else would have you staring off into space like you've been drugged? Right, spill the beans. Who is she? What's her name and—more to the point—what does she look like? Is she a babe?'

Conall dug his hands deep into his pockets, then walked slowly across to the huge plate-glass window. Staring out at the teeming city below, with its traffic fumes and furious honking drivers, he sucked in a deep breath. 'She's someone who works in the London office. Her name is Morgen and she looks like a raven-haired angel. Oh, and she's definitely a babe. Satisfied?'

'I would be if I was so lucky to meet such a dream!' Rubbing his hand over his thinning brown hair, Mike shook his head in wonder. 'The women of New York are going to go into mourning when they find out, you realise that?'

'Can't play the field for ever.'

'No,' Mike agreed, 'but a man can have a damn good time trying! You sure she's the one?'

Conall had no hesitation in replying. 'She's the one, all right. From now on, my friend...I'm a one-woman man.'

His flight was delayed. Delayed! Morgen stared up at the blinking green digits on the Arrivals board and bitterly swallowed down her rising frustration.

Six days he'd been gone, and she hadn't had a decent night's sleep since. She'd been prowling the kitchen in the early hours of the morning, making tea, listening to the radio, painting her nails—anything to try and divert her thoughts from thinking about Conall. She'd known she had it bad when she'd put the jelly mould she'd filled with Neesha's favourite raspberry jelly in the oven instead of the fridge, and thrown out her morning's post with the rubbish. And only this afternoon her poor mother had told her to make an appointment with the doctor because she was convinced she was coming down with something viral!

Pushing her fingers through her hair, Morgen sighed dramatically, then reluctantly marched over to a row of chairs and sat down. On one side of her was a youth dressed in a shiny tracksuit and a baseball cap, listening to music on his headphones, and on the other a middle-aged blonde woman in tailored black trousers and a boxy red jacket. Her long red nails fascinated Morgen as, momentarily distracted, she watched them dip in and out of her brown suede handbag for her make-up mirror, then her lipstick.

Catching her glance, the woman smiled. Her make-up was picture-perfect, and her teeth very even and white. It made Morgen remember that she hadn't been able to devote the time she would have liked to making herself beautiful for Conall. She'd had to rush to give Neesha her tea before driving her over to her mother's, then dash back to the house for a quick change out of her working clothes into jeans and a cotton shirt before driving to Heathrow Airport to meet Conall's plane. Truth to tell, she couldn't remember if she'd even stopped to brush her hair.

'Meeting someone?' the woman asked her politely.

'Yes.' Her answer came out in a breathless rush, and Morgen willed herself to stay calm. Not easy when her stomach kept doing cartwheels every time she thought about seeing Conall.

'Anybody special?'

Only the love of my life, Morgen thought silently, her heartbeat going crazy. 'Yes, he's special.'

'I thought so.'

'Why's that?' Curious, Morgen tipped her head.

'I've been watching you walk up and down with that look on your face every time you glance at the Arrivals board for the past half-hour now.'

'Oh?' Discomfited at the thought that her feelings were apparently transparent to a total stranger, Morgen twisted her hands together in her lap. 'What look do you mean, exactly?'

The woman's perfectly arched eyebrows lifted a little to accompany her gently knowing smile. 'The look that a woman gets on her face when she's in love and can't wait to see the man she's in love with.'

'Oh.' Morgen dropped her shoulders, untwisted her hands and looped her hair behind her ear. 'Is it so obvious?'

'Only to a kindred spirit. My husband Graham and I just celebrated our twentieth wedding anniversary, and I'm still as head over heels in love with him as I was the day we met.'

At Morgen's interested glance, the woman introduced herself as Faye Mortimer, then confided that her marriage to Graham was in fact her second marriage—she'd divorced her first husband because he'd been a womaniser and an abuser. The fact was, she continued, she'd never

dreamed she would get a second chance at happiness after everything she'd been through. It just went to show
that if you didn't allow yourself to become all bitter and
twisted about love, love paid back your trust tenfold.

An hour later Morgen had shared her own marriage
disaster with Faye, right down to the revelation that
Simon had walked out on her when she was pregnant,
then blithely washed his hands of both her and their child
because he was convinced he had married beneath him.

For quite a while there, Morgen realised, she *had* been
bitter and twisted. Right up until the moment she'd
known she had fallen for Conall O'Brien, in fact. When
that had been exactly she couldn't rightly say, but maybe
it was the time he had followed her and Neesha to the
Tumble Drum, bought them drinks and sat with her
watching Neesha play for the rest of the afternoon—the
whole time looking as if there was nowhere he'd rather
be on the planet than with them.

Glancing at her watch, hardly believing that so much
time had passed, Morgen turned apologetically to Faye.
'I've got to see if there's any more news about his flight,'
she explained. 'It's been so nice talking to you, Faye. I'd
love to think that in twenty years' time I'll still be with
the man I love, celebrating our wedding anniversary.'

Faye smiled. 'If this Conall of yours is anything like
the way you've described him, I've no doubt you'll be
popping the champagne corks on your twentieth and
looking forward to the next twenty years with your
grandchildren. Take care, Morgen. It was nice meeting
you too.'

Twenty minutes later Morgen was peering over the
heads and shoulders of the waiting crowd pressed round
the Arrivals barrier, trying to catch a glimpse of the tall,

broad-shouldered and devastatingly handsome man she loved. She spotted him straight away, excitement jamming her breath in her throat and making her heart pound. Head and shoulders above nearly everybody else who spilled onto the polished walkway, he was easily the most eye-catching male in the area, and Morgen couldn't suppress the shudder of anticipation that shot through her at the thought of being alone with him later.

Pushing her way through the throng of people at the barrier, she forgot that she usually liked to keep her emotions well under wraps, that in public she always liked to maintain a low profile, that in her book public displays of affection in general were undignified. She raced onto the walkway, calling his name.

Stopping right where he was, the trenchcoat he'd worn in a cold and rainy New York before boarding the plane folded over his arm, and carrying his leather holdall, Conall could hardly believe his eyes when he saw Morgen hurrying towards him. Letting his bag drop to the floor, he simply stood and stared. She was dressed in faded blue jeans, a white cotton shirt and a black suede jacket, with her long dark hair flying out behind her, and she was everything he'd ever dreamed of finding in a woman and more. God how he'd missed her! He'd made the flight from New York to London many times in the past, but it had never seemed to take as long as it had today. Now he was back home, and Morgen was waiting to greet him. Just as he'd hoped and dreamed she would be.

Sprinting the last couple of feet that separated them, without hesitation Morgen threw herself into his arms. Conall almost stumbled with the force of her embrace, the air suddenly leaving his lungs in a powerful 'oomph!' But still he held onto her tight, raining kisses down on her fresh sweet-smelling hair, then desperately seeking her mouth in a hard and hungry kiss that fuelled the longing inside him to fever-pitch and made him nigh on desperate to be alone with her just as soon as he could. The woman was temptation with a capital 'T', and Conall was helpless to resist such potent charms. He was only flesh and blood after all…

'I love you.'

'What?'

Pretending not to hear, Conall stared into her beguiling green eyes, got lost in them for a second or two, then surfaced again with a grin.

'I said I love you—and I want to marry you!' Morgen was sliding her hand up his shirt, holding onto his waist with her free hand, careless that they were receiving highly interested stares from passing disembarking passengers, as well as the public awaiting their arrival. 'I couldn't wait to tell you.'

'So I see.'

'I'm sorry I made you wait for an answer. I wasn't trying to play hard to get.' Planting a brief loving kiss at the side of his jaw, she seemed to think that wasn't enough, and planted another one for good measure at the corner of his mouth. 'I just wanted to have the chance to talk to Neesha about it…about us getting married. Do you mind?'

He wanted it to be right with Morgen's little girl, Conall realised. He didn't want her to think he was going to walk into their lives and claim all her mother's attention for himself. It was important he let her know he cared for her too, and would do anything he could to always keep her feeling safe and loved.

Slipping his arm around Morgen's shoulders, he shook

his head. 'I don't mind at all. I'm glad you did. And was she…was she okay about it?'

Her answering smile was like the kiss of moonlight on a summer garden…sublime. 'She was fine about it. She even helped her nana bake you a cake. I've got it waiting at home, for us to enjoy with a cup of tea.'

'Home?' Conall's blue eyes narrowed.

'My house. You will stay with us until we find something together, won't you? I know it's quite a small place, but it's warm and cosy. Or if you'd prefer to stay at your sister's, I'll understand.'

Conall was surprised at the flash of anxiety in her lovely eyes. 'Your house will be just fine, my angel. As long as we can be together, right?'

It was exactly the answer Morgen wanted to hear.

'And as soon as we get five minutes I want to show you the plans I've been working on.'

'What plans are those?'

'For the house I'm going to build us—you, me and Neesha.'

'Oh, Conall!'

Once again her embrace produced that 'oomph' sound from his chest, but as the last passers-by moved slowly ahead of them Conall found he couldn't wait to kiss his wife-to-be again…and again. By the time they reached the Arrivals barrier nearly everyone else had cleared the area, but the pair of them hardly noticed. They were much too preoccupied with each other to care.

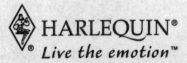

eHARLEQUIN.com

The Ultimate Destination for Women's Fiction

The eHarlequin.com online community is *the* place to share opinions, thoughts and feelings!

- Joining the community is easy, fun and **FREE!**

- Connect with **other romance fans** on our message boards.

- Meet your **favorite authors** without leaving home!

- **Share opinions** on books, movies, celebrities…and *more!*

Here's what our members say:

"I love the friendly and helpful atmosphere filled with support and humor."
—Texanna (eHarlequin.com member)

"Is this the place for me, or what? There is nothing I love more than 'talking' books, especially with fellow readers who are reading the same ones I am."
—Jo Ann (eHarlequin.com member)

Join today by visiting
www.eHarlequin.com!

HARLEQUIN®
INTRIGUE®

WE'LL LEAVE YOU BREATHLESS!

If you've been looking for thrilling tales of contemporary passion and sensuous love stories with taut, edge-of-the-seat suspense—then you'll love Harlequin Intrigue!

Every month, you'll meet six new heroes who are guaranteed to make your spine tingle and your pulse pound. With them you'll enter into the exciting world of Harlequin Intrigue— where your life is on the line and so is your heart!

THAT'S INTRIGUE— ROMANTIC SUSPENSE AT ITS BEST!

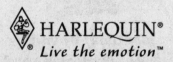

HARLEQUIN®
Live the emotion™

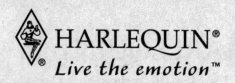

HARLEQUIN®
Live the emotion™

Upbeat,
All-American Romances

Romantic Comedy

Harlequin Historicals®

Historical,
Romantic Adventure

HARLEQUIN®
INTRIGUE

Romantic Suspense

HARLEQUIN ROMANCE®

The essence of
modern romance

HARLEQUIN®
Presents

Seduction and passion
guaranteed

Emotional,
Exciting, Unexpected

Sassy, Sexy, Seductive!

eHARLEQUIN.com

The Ultimate Destination for Women's Fiction

Calling all aspiring writers!
Learn to craft the perfect romance novel
with our useful tips and tools:

- Take advantage of our **Romance Novel Critique Service** for detailed advice from romance professionals.

- Use our **message boards** to connect with writers, published authors and editors.

- Enter our **Writing Round Robin—** you could be published online!

- Learn many tools of the writer's trade from editors and authors in our **On Writing** section!

- **Writing guidelines** for Harlequin or Silhouette novels—what our editors *really* look for.

Learn more about romance writing from the experts—
visit www.eHarlequin.com today!

passionate powerful provocative love stories

Silhouette Desire delivers strong heroes, spirited heroines and compelling love stories.

Desire features your favorite authors, including

Annette Broadrick, Ann Major, Anne McAllister and Cait London.

Passionate, powerful and provocative romances *guaranteed!*

For superlative authors, sensual stories and sexy heroes, choose Silhouette Desire.

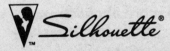

passionate powerful provocative love stories

SDGEN0